Academy

Rainforest Rescue

RIAH RAJANI

Illustrated by: Shalini Soni Mazumdar

Wonder House

Printed 2023

 Wonder House

(An imprint of Prakash Books Pvt. Ltd.)

Wonder House Books
Corporate & Editorial Office
113-A, 1st Floor, Ansari Road,
Daryaganj, New Delhi-110002

Tel +91 11 2324 7062-65

ISBN: 978-93-5440-855-7

Printed in India

*To Mum and Dad, my amazing,
loving pets – Tisa, Pip, Leo, and Xena, and
my awesome best friends. All of you have
encouraged me to do my best, inspired me, and
believed in me every step of the way.*

Contents

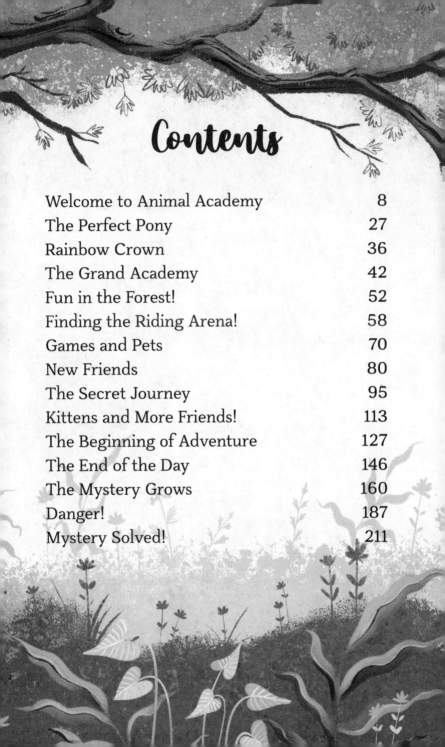

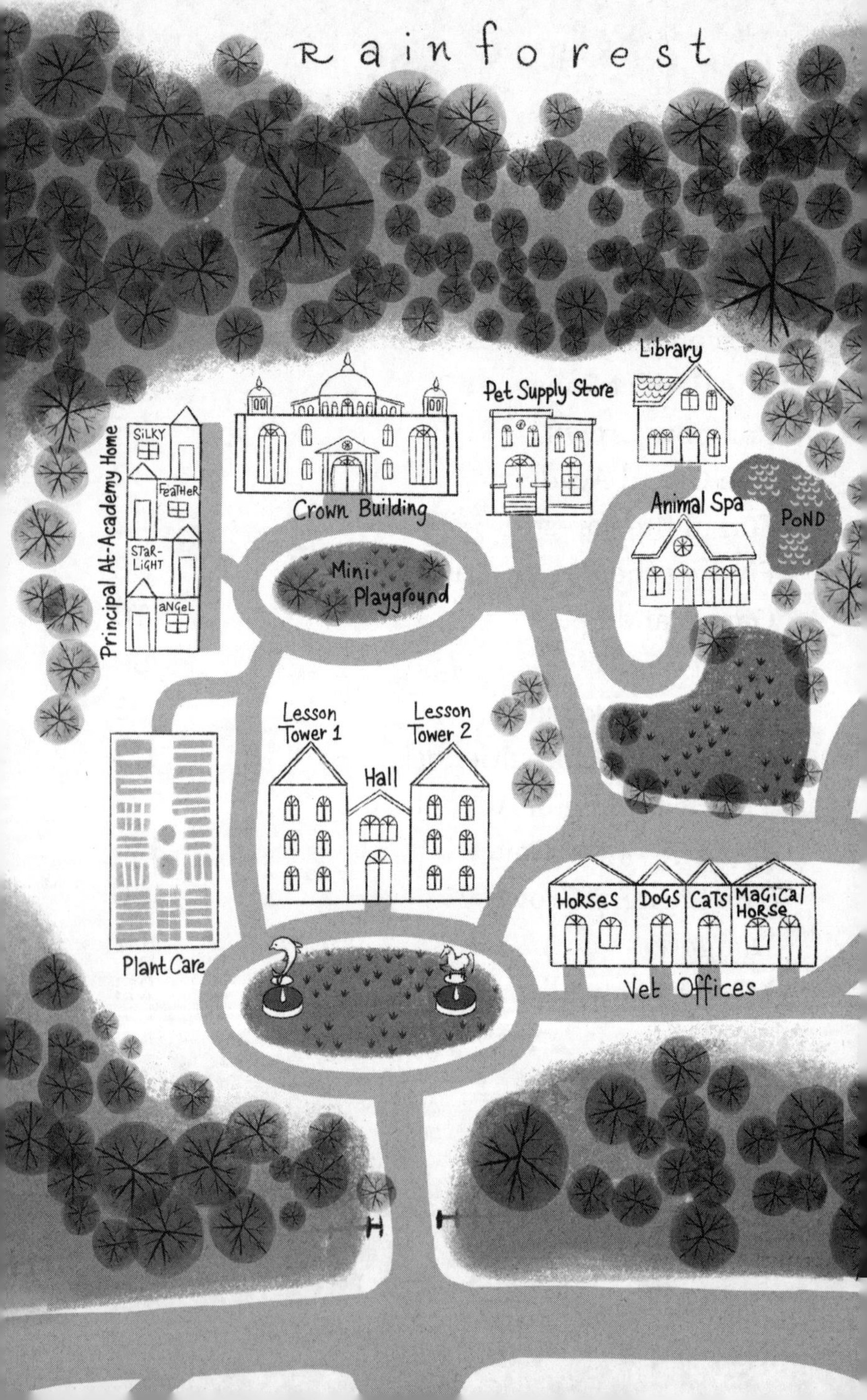

Rainforest

Library

Pet Supply Store

Crown Building

Animal Spa

PoND

Principal At-Academy Home

SILKY

FeaTHeR

STAR-LiGHT

aNGeL

Mini Playground

Lesson Tower 1

Lesson Tower 2

Hall

Plant Care

HoRSeS   DoGS   CaTs   MAGICAL HoRSE

Vet Offices

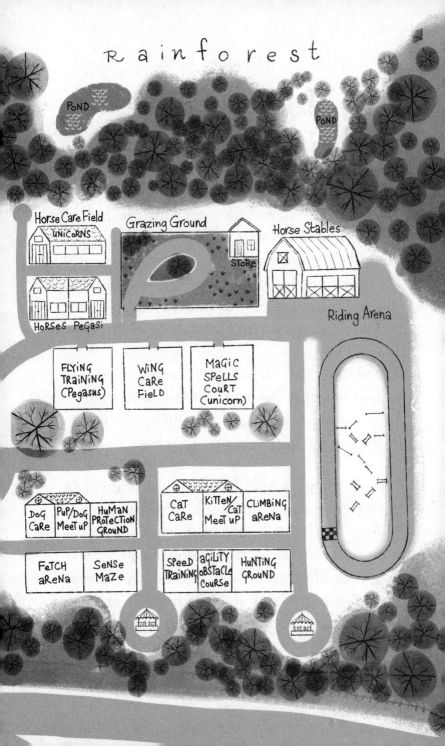

Chapter 1

Welcome to Animal Academy

As Emily entered the gorgeous grounds of Animal Academy, she felt a rush of pure delight. "It's amazing," she breathed, gazing at the sparkling buildings, trees, and fountains. "It's been my lifelong dream to come. I can't believe I'm finally here!"

She skipped to a beautiful, rainbow-coloured banner that said, "Welcome to Animal Academy!" and beamed, thinking of how lucky she was to be able to come to her dream school.

"The Academy is breathtaking," she whispered to herself, amazed at how lovely the gardens looked. Fountains sculpted as various animals were scattered around the freshly cut grass. Star magnolia, cherry blossom, and dogwood trees framed the grounds. Rabbits hopped around, either weaving through daphne bushes, or leaping over one another.

Emily knelt down to pet one. She giggled as her fingers touched its soft grey fur, and then tickled the cute, furry little thing between its ears.

"It does look incredible, doesn't it?" her mother said, placing a hand gently on Emily's shoulder. "Your older sister Olivia loved it here, and so did I, when I was your age. It still holds the same fresh, happy atmosphere."

Emily agreed. "It does, doesn't it, Mum?" She felt butterflies in her tummy, unable to imagine staying at such a grandiose school.

"It sure does. You must show Thunder the fountain with a sculpture of a horse. It looks like him," winked Emily's mum.

Emily giggled. "I bet I'll enjoy practically every second here. But I will miss you and Dad a little." She knew she wasn't too sad about leaving her home for a year or two. She had Thunder, she was positive that she would make a bunch of new friends, and she also had new teachers. Besides, postcards do exist and she could write to her family any time she liked!

"The whole school is so pretty. Even though I haven't seen even half of it," she told her mum.

Then she paused and bit her lip. "You know, I'm over the moon to be here, but I really do hope I make a lot of new friends. I'll miss our home and my old friends, like Stella and Katie. But, honestly, looking at how welcoming this place is, I feel I'll settle in with everybody else." She grinned. "And I promise I'll work hard in all my lessons. I bet Thunder will too. Speaking of which, where is Thunder?"

"Your father is going to get him out of his trailer," replied Emily's mum. As she spoke, a light brown stallion pranced towards Emily. "I got Thunder out," Emily's father puffed, looking a little flushed.

"I . . . guess I'll go in now," Emily said, her tummy tying itself in knots. "I'll miss you two, but I remember reading that the Academy lets you visit your parents each weekend if your house isn't too far away."

"That'll be us. We're really close by," Emily's dad said, patting Thunder. "Thunder's a good boy too. Bring him over any time you please."

Emily's mum raised an eyebrow. "We'll see about Thunder. But, Emily, have the best time ever. And do write to us and your friends." She smiled gently.

"You'll settle in in no time," Emily's dad said reassuringly.

"Now go on," her mum said, patting Emily.

"Have a lot of fun, work hard, and make tons of friends. Bye!"

"Bye!"

As much as Emily was sad to leave behind her parents, home, and old friends, she was actually quite excited for the first day at this awesome school. She hugged her parents, waved, and skipped to a group of girls.

"Hello!" a tall, friendly looking girl said cheerfully.

"My name is Violette. I'm guessing you're new here. Never seen you before."

"I am new here," Emily replied. Violette seems nice. "You're not?"

"You know, everyone here stays for three years. I came a year ago," said Violette. "I'll call a teacher to assign you to a Crown, which is like a dorm. Wait by the dogwood tree, please."

Emily nodded and stood under the tree, beaming from ear to ear. Thunder whickered and nuzzled her cheek. Emily sighed with pleasure and remembered how she had met him.

She had always wanted a pet, and then, on the week she turned nine, her dream had come true! It was the best day of my life, Emily remembered. At Sunshine Meadows, I met Thunder. I was crossing the bridge, and a wild stallion caught my eye. He looked perfect.

Emily smiled at the memory of her going up to him, smiling, and petting him. There he stood—a tall, light brown stallion with black hooves, and a mane and tail which was a bit darker than his coat, braided with emerald-green rubber bands. She remembered Thunder's ecstatic face when he had seen her for the first time.

We're just going to have more fun now that we're here, she thought, looking around the Academy. On the first day she had met Thunder, Emily had mounted onto him happily. As he had pranced around the meadow and across the rivers, she'd felt the wind blowing gently on her face.

Emily remembered that, after riding Thunder for half an hour, her parents had told her that it was time to go home. When they had come up to the bridge, they had seen her and Thunder having immense fun. "Well, we can't just leave him without his new best friend, can we?" Emily's father had said.

"I suppose not," Emily remembered her mother say with a twinkle in her eye.

Letting Thunder canter the whole way to their home, Emily's family wondered how they would manage to keep a horse.

Emily remembered deciding to let Thunder stay in the backyard until her cousin Kate suggested a school called Animal Academy. Kate had said that this school was ideal for learning pet care. That got Emily so eager.

After asking her parents and meeting their approval, Emily told Thunder about the Academy and about how strongly she felt about enrolling there. "Certainly! Animal Academy sounds so cool," Thunder had told her excitedly.

Then, after a few months, Emily received a neat little envelope in the mail saying that . . . Animal Academy had decided to enroll her in the school! She and Thunder were thrilled.

Emily glanced at Thunder, her light brown stallion, trotting behind her. She stroked his braided mane. "We are going to have so much fun!" she told him, her heart glowing with pleasure as she looked around. Thunder nickered as he saw a teacher coming towards them.

"Hello!" a lady greeted cheerfully, waving, and hurrying over to Emily and Thunder. She had golden-orange hair tied in a neat bun, was wearing a sky-blue shirt with pale green culottes. She smiled kindly as she said, "I'm Ms. Williams, your horse, cat, and dog affection teacher." She shook hands warmly with Emily and patted Thunder. "And you are?"

Emily had been so mesmerized by the beauty around that she hardly heard Ms. Williams' words. Guessing what the teacher had said, she said, "I'm. . . I'm Emily. I have a horse."

"Thunder," Emily's horse said, eyes twinkling, "the most awesome name in the world."

"Amazing to meet you, Thunder and Emily," said Ms. Williams.

"Good to meet you, too," said Emily politely. "I love Animal Academy."

"Can you please tell us more about this wonderful school?" Thunder asked, looking around.

"Certainly! To be in Animal Academy, you must have one pet. It can either be a horse, a unicorn, a pegasus, a cat, or a dog," Ms. Williams explained.

"Where in the Academy am I?" wondered Emily.

"We are next to the Mini Playground. If you turn around, you will see the building where you will stay," said Ms. Williams.

Emily nodded and turned to look where Ms. Williams was pointing.

"Animal Academy is on a vast patch of land with a rainforest next to it. Our curriculum is the same as in any other academic school. We have all sorts of lessons that teach you how to care for and befriend your pets, too" Ms. Williams went on.

"You come to the Academy when you are seven or above, and the main goal you need to put your mind to is learning how to take care of your pet. The Academy's grounds contain many other domesticated animals, as you can see, Emily."

Ms. Williams said as she took out a clipboard and pen from her shoulder bag and nodded towards a family of wild rabbits frolicking in and out of a patch of dahlias, "You can befriend them, but not take them to your room. Remember, the main care you need to provide is for Thunder."

"Of course."

Ms. Williams bent down as a puppy came racing

towards her. "Oh hello, Fern. Emily, Thunder, this is my puppy."

Emily looked down at the puppy and smiled. "Hello!" she said.

"Go on, Fern. You can greet the students over there," she pointed to a group of chattering girls.

"I like Fern. He is so well-mannered." Emily looked lovingly at Thunder and added, "Thunder is incredibly good at jumping. He also runs amazingly fast and—"

Thunder interrupted, "I do hope there are riding lessons."

"How nice of you to praise your pet, Emily," Ms. Williams remarked. "And yes, there are riding lessons."

"Oh, thank you. Am I going to stay with other children or by myself?"

"You will be in a Crown with other girls. A Crown is like a dormitory. A Crown is made up of many Diamonds, which are separate rooms that each of you will stay in," Ms. Williams told them as another teacher with blonde hair walked up to them. "Hello, I am Ms. Smith. I am the riding teacher," she said.

"I am Emily."

"Nice to meet you. May I take your horse to the stables? That's where he will stay. You can go to see him there anytime. Once you have reached the stables, feel free to ride him around, exploring the Academy as you go."

"Sure!"

Ms. Smith gently took Thunder away, talking to him in a comforting voice.

"Emily, you will be in Rainbow Crown with a few other girls. Ah, and there is Abby, one of the girls in your Crown," Ms. Williams said, looking at the girl who was stepping out of a car with a cat in hand. Emily noticed that Abby had orange hair, freckles on her face, and dark blue eyes. "And this is Isla," Ms. Williams smiled at a girl wearing a bright pink top with a green skirt, both patterned with daisies. Emily smiled at her. She loved daisies. They were her favourite! Isla waved to Emily. "Hey," she said, a huge smile on her face. "I am Isla. I have a pegasus! I bet he will fly fast. He is the best! His name is Pocket. No, sorry, it's Rock Knit, or . . ." She sighed. "I just can't remember . . . I'd go for Locket. You know what? I'll go right now to check with him."

"Isla!" Ms. Williams tried to sound firm but couldn't help but softly chuckle. "You are not to go to the stables and ask your pet what his name is."

Isla is so amusing, Emily thought, giggling. His name might be Rocket. It does rhyme with Pocket!

Emily suddenly heard her favourite song. She realized that somebody was humming a tune, but it wasn't Isla or Ms. Williams.

"That's beautiful, Victoria," Ms. Williams said to the girl standing at a little distance to them.

Victoria was carrying a guitar, violin, and microphone. "Thank you, Ms. Williams!" She kept her instruments carefully on the ground and began to walk up to Emily and Ms. Williams. "Wait for me," said a girl while dragging her heavy luggage bag. She huffed and puffed while walking beside Victoria. "I'm Lily," she said. "And this is my best friend, Victoria."

"We live in the same neighbourhood and have been friends for as long as we can remember," said Victoria.

Emily gave them both a shy smile. Victoria and Lily looked like best friends. She hoped that she'd have a best friend soon, too. All the girls she could see looked very friendly. Still, Emily didn't know who to go up to!

The last girl in Rainbow Crown was a girl with glossy, dark purple glasses, and a lilac backpack. "Hello," she said.

"Oh, there you are, Ivy," Ms. Williams said. "I thought you were going to be late! Anyhow, you have come to the right group. These are the girls in your Crown."

"Hello, Ivy!" Victoria sang.

"Hey," Lily greeted.

"Hi!" chorused Isla and Abby.

"Hello," Emily said, blushing.

Ivy waved to everyone and stood by Emily.

"Hi!" she said to Emily.

"Hi, Ivy," Emily said with a smile. "I'm Emily."

"Emily? Nice name," said Ivy. "Are you new too?"

"You bet," said Emily. "The older girls seem nice too, though."

"Alright, everybody, please stop talking. You will have lots of free time between lessons to do so," Ms. Williams said, clapping her hands twice for silence. "Now, Ivy, Emily, Victoria, Lily, and Isla, soon you will need to go to the stables to meet your pets again, and—oh dear!" Ms. Williams stepped back as Abby's cat almost leapt out of her arms. "Abby, since you have a cat, you won't be going to the stables."

Ms. Williams handed each girl a map of the area. "Do you all understand? You can use this to find your way to the stables. It's over there," she pointed a finger in the direction of the stables. The girls nodded, opening their maps.

"Abby, you will go to the pet collection building to buy all the amenities your cat needs, including scratching posts, litter boxes, feeding bowls, and the tracking accessory," Ms. Williams told her, and pointed to an 'L' shaped building with bold words: Pet Store and Collection. "I'll go with you because you are the only one without a horse, unicorn, or pegasus. Do you want me to hold your cat while we head there?"

"Yes, please, thank you," said Abby. She gently handed her squirming cat to Ms. Williams.

Emily liked Ms. Williams.

Ms. Williams lovingly stroked the cat, and then turned to Abby and asked, "What is your cat's name?"

Abby looked surprised. "Oh, I haven't named him yet. I'll name him once I get to know him better!" She paused for a few seconds, then looked at Ms. Williams and said, "Well, he is not a pet cat, that's all I know. I adopted him from the sidewalk near my house. He is really cute and brilliant at climbing."

Hearing this, Abby's cat made an adorable face and purred.

Ms. Williams shook her head and laughed. "Okay, well the rest of you better head to the stables."

I wonder if Ivy has got a horse like me, Emily thought as the girls from Rainbow Crown started to walk towards the stables. And what about everyone else's pets? Oh, I can't wait to meet them!

Ms. Williams and Abby started walking towards Pet Store and Collection. They had taken a few steps when Ms. Williams suddenly stopped. She turned around and said to the girls, "Oh, in the stables you will meet the riding teacher, Ms. Smith," she reminded them. "Now, you better get going! You don't want to be late!" With that, she hurried off to another group of girls with Abby following behind.

"I have a unicorn," Victoria sang, skipping on the path.

"Sweet. Mine is a pegasus," said Isla. "A marvellous pegasus with magic wings!" she added, spreading her arms wide.

"Mine, too," Lily chipped in, laughing.

"Isla! You know pegasi don't have magical wings," Ivy giggled. "I can't wait to get to the stables."

"Me neither," Lily said, excited.

"Here's to tons more fun, with our horses!" Emily cheered.

Chapter 2

The Perfect Pony

"Hmm," murmured Ivy, half-listening, and studying the map intently. "So, we are here." She pointed her finger at a small path near the Mini Playground, connecting two vast squares of land together. There were many more, even bigger squares of land next to them.

"Come on, follow me! I know where we should go!" Ivy declared in excitement.

Emily and the others started off. After walking for a minute, they reached some palm trees. "Is this a sign that we're close?" she asked, puzzled.

"Ha ha! Actually, this is a Gloss-Vine coconut tree! Quite rare," remarked Isla. She felt the tree with her palm and went to the back of it. "It says here we have about five more minutes of walking!" came a shout. Isla reappeared with a baby coconut and a sign that said:

"Welcome! You are five minutes away from the stables. Turn right to head to the stables. Turn left to head to Pet Store and Collection," read Victoria.

"Remember: do not go into the rainforest without a teacher's approval. Have a great day, students!" continued Lily. "Well, that was helpful!"

Ivy nodded. "Agreed. Let's go right."

Humming and talking, the girls of Rainbow Crown were near the stables in no time. The right fork which they had taken was relatively close to the left one, and the girls had passed Abby several times.

"Oh!" Isla suddenly exclaimed when they were close to the stables. She pointed to the pet store in the distance. "There's Abby and Ms. Williams!" she said, pointing to the two of them running around, trying to catch Abby's cat from darting away.

Isla squinted. "I think Abby's cat is trying to get away. He looks lovely though! Oh my, I remember

what type of cat he is. It was written about in my nature and wildlife book."

She paused and knitted her brow. "He's a . . . a Tabby cat, I think," she told them, grinning. "Just a second. I think I'll go meet the Tabby." She ran up to Abby. Emily and the rest of the girls could hear her exclamations.

"Hey, Abby! I love that cat!" Isla said. "What's his name? How old is he? Oh, you are so lucky! I love him! Oh, his ears are so cute! I love the look in his eyes! His meows are sweet! He's so graceful! Wow, he looks elegant! His tail is so . . . so long! Beautiful—I'm jealous!"

Abby's cat purred, jumped into his owner's arms, and meowed at Isla, looking friendly. "This kitty is too cute. I won't be a minute!" Isla called out to the girls.

"Yes," Lily called back, giving Isla an affectionate smile. "Don't be!" Then Lily said to the others, "She'll come. Well, I sure hope she will! Come on, Rainbow Crown! Let's go!"

The girls walked on a turquoise path and reached the stables. There were so many horses there, but not just them. "UNICORNS! PEGASI!" exclaimed Emily.
Emily rushed over to the horses, separating from almost the whole group, except for Ivy. "Wow! You have got a horse, too?" Ivy and Emily said together. They really couldn't contain their excitement any longer.

Emily eyed the remaining horses.
Where is my horse?

After searching for a few seconds, Emily's eyes finally spotted her tall stallion. Warmth spread through Emily as she gazed at Thunder.

Emily rushed over to Thunder's stall and enveloped him in a hug. Thunder whinnied and reared up, clearly happy to see Emily. "Emily! I'm so glad you came."

"Hi, Thunder! I'm happy to see you, too," Emily said shyly, as she patted him. On the door of the stall was a plate. It, of course, said: Thunder. "I am going to do my best to be the perfect partner," Emily vowed, brushing her horse's hair out of his eyes fondly.

Thunder closed his eyes and brought his nose close to Emily's. "You're amazing, already," said Thunder. "We'll be best friends forever! I can almost feel that we'll go on tons of exciting adventures together," he went on, delighted. "Now, um, please get me out of this!" He bucked, making Emily jump.

"Sure!" Emily giggled. She picked up a bright

silver key near the stall and dusted it. While she went on to unlock the door, she heard squeals of delight as other girls met their pets.

The stall door opened with a click as Emily unlocked it. Thunder took a deep breath as he trotted out, halting in the partition. He played with Emily's hair and then began to circle her, making her laugh.

Emily and Thunder were startled by the sudden sound of footsteps.

It was Isla! "Sorry I'm late," she panted, dripping with sweat. Her blonde hair looked like a mop over her head. "Abby's cat's name is Lie Thing, by the way. Um,

I am a bit forgetful, so forgive me if the cat isn't Lie Bing." She winked and jogged off to the unicorn and pegasi's side of the stables.

Emily stroked Thunder's mane as a calm silence covered the stables.

"I know this is sort of strange," Thunder said, breaking the silence, "but would you want to ride me now?"

His face lit up when Emily exclaimed, "Yes! Yes! Oh, I'd love to!"

Emily had only briefly ridden before. She was certain it would be easy this time around, too.

Emily tried to jump onto Thunder, though it was only after her fourth attempt that she was able to jump high enough to land on Thunder's back. She clung onto his mane and commanded, "Forward!"

Thunder's eyes twinkled and he neighed so loud that the sound echoed in the stables. "I'm not a robot," he snorted. "I'm a horse! A stallion. A majestic leaper, prancer, galloper, and trotter!" He laughed. "You need to gesture me to move where you want me to go."

Emily placed her hands firmly on Thunder. She looked around. "Let's exit the stables?" she suggested.

"Sure thing!" Thunder obediently trotted to the door and nudged it open with his muzzle, and quickly galloped out into the open. Emily inhaled in contentment as the wind blew around them. The branches of the trees were swaying in the cool breeze. "That duck pond over there looks nice," Thunder nickered. "Is that Ivy feeding the ducklings?" "Oh, wow! It looks like her, and," Emily paused and squinted, "there's her pony! I'd love to meet her."

"Me, too! Come on," Thunder pranced towards them.

As Thunder slowed down to a trot, Emily realized that even though she had been slightly nervous riding him, prancing had been quite fun.

Once Emily and Thunder reached the pond, they discovered that Ivy had a palomino pony with a wavy, cream mane and tail. "This is my pony, Lavender," Ivy whispered. "She's the best pony ever. Well," Ivy blushed in embarrassment, "she and Thunder, of course. I've ridden Lavender six times before. She lived in the field in my house. Now, she lives in her stable."

"Lavender is really cool, Ivy," said Emily.

"I'm so glad we're here," whispered Thunder, nuzzling Emily's cheek.

"Me, too," Emily murmured back. "And I'm so glad you're with me!"

Chapter 3
Rainbow Crown

Lavender neighed and smiled at Thunder. "Hello. I'm Lavender and I'm four," she said shyly.

"I'm Thunder and I'm the same age as you!"

Soon, the rest of Rainbow Crown strode to the pond, and they all chattered excitedly with each other. Making friends hasn't been so hard after all! Emily thought. She soon met other girls' pets as well.

Lily had an indigo pegasus with a teal mane. Her wings had turquoise butterflies and snowflakes patterned on them. On her flank there was a neon crescent moon and under it were tiny stars. The pegasus had no horn, but Emily noticed that on one of her rainbow hooves was a neon pink crescent, just like the one on her flank.

"This is Moon, my pegasus!" Lily beamed. Moon swished her mane and her eyes shone.

"We are going to have the best time ever! Lily's the best!" Moon said.

"Emily is also the best, like Lily," said Thunder, swishing his brown tail. Emily's tummy twisted and she blushed. She knew she should say thank you, but what if she wasn't the best rider ever?

Emily blushed even harder, but her embarrassment was forgotten when Isla strode in with her pegasus "Hocket", "Locket", or "Pocket".

Isla had a bright orange pegasus who had a sprinkling of golden stars on his flank. Beneath his mane was a swirly pattern of red and gold. He had twinkling eyes and short eyelashes. "Here's my pegasus, Pocket," Isla explained. Her pegasus looked at Isla blankly, stifling a giggle. "I'm Rocket," he announced. "But I like the name Pocket!"

"He flies really fast!" said Isla dramatically. Rocket nudged her. "Um, to be honest I haven't seen

Rocket fly. But I guess he flies fast," Isla said. Rocket laughed lightly. "You guessed right, Isla. I do."

They all chatted for a few minutes and then spotted Victoria. She was leading a buttercup-coloured unicorn with a dark teal mane. On his cheek, he had an indigo and pink planet. He had magenta eyes and a playful look on his face. "Here is Saturn, my unicorn," Victoria said. "He's amazing, isn't he? He is so colourful!"

Saturn was humming a happy tune, just like Victoria.

The field was now filled with the sound of warm laughter of the students and their pets. After some time, everyone heard a loud clap. "Alright!" spoke a teacher. She was petite and had confident, hazel eyes. Her smile was welcoming as the students filed past. "I am your riding teacher, Ms. Smith. You must already have a map of the Academy. Remember, the riding arenas that I teach in are open to all, almost all the time. Except when classes are taking place, only horses can enter." She waved to the girls and their horses, saying, "Off you go!"

Emily straddled Thunder and pet him behind the ears, happily.

The students got ready to ride their pets further, but Emily chose to go to Rainbow Crown. I wonder what Rainbow Crown looks like! Emily wondered. I cannot wait to explore! But then she remembered that it would mean leaving Thunder in the stables! Emily didn't know what to do. She felt torn. Thunder meant a lot to her, and she wanted to spend every minute she had with him. I'll stay with Thunder, she decided.

Emily led Thunder near the Crowns. They reached a small park filled with trees, flowers, a cobblestone path, and lovely emerald-green grass.

Pointing her finger at the map, Emily said, "So, Thunder, we are at the Mini Playground, where we were before going to the stables." She paused. "Where do you want to go?"

Thunder looked thoughtful. "The Riding Arena," he decided. "The one that Ms. Smith told us about. Please!"

Emily didn't have the heart to tell Thunder that she would prefer being in the Mini Playground, cafeteria, or even the Pet Spa, watching puppies getting massages.

"Sure thing," Emily said. She didn't feel like riding but told herself that she had to try it if she wanted to be Thunder's best friend. "I . . . can't wait."

"I want to see everything," Thunder declared.

"Sure! We'll have loads of fun today," Emily said, hopping off Thunder's back. "What classes do we have tomorrow?"

Thunder whinnied, looking confused. "I don't know. I'm not allowed in the Diamonds, and I haven't seen your schedule."

Emily giggled. "I'll check with my friends," she said. "They told me they'd be going to the Diamonds. I wonder what the Diamonds are like!"

Thunder neighed. "I bet they're as awesome as the stables."

Emily hoped not; a room stacked with hay bales and troughs? "I . . . bet they are. Now, let's go to the Riding Arena!"

Chapter 4
The Grand Academy

"**W**e need to go through the back door of the stables to get to the Arena," Emily announced. She giggled as Thunder tickled her with his tail. "And once we're there we can—" she broke off mid-sentence as Thunder neighed. "Hang on!" He swerved past her and bolted to the stables.

"Thunds!" Emily called, puzzled as she watched Thunder push his way into the stables again. Why did her horse want to race away from her?

"Come back, you frisky thing!" she hollered. "I won't be able to catch up with you!" She darted to the stables.

Once she had shoved the heavy door open and strode into the stables, she found Thunder in the barn with Lavender and Ivy. The horses were standing close to each other and chit-chatting. "One second," Thunder told Lavender, smiling, and then walked towards Emily.

"Hey there, Emily, what's up? I thought you'd never reach," Thunder winked.

"It's the only two legs rule," Emily grinned.

"Well," Thunder said, "good for you I can introduce a new four-legged. Basically, Lavender is my new friend."

Emily patted Thunder's mane. "That's great!" she said, her eyes sparkling and dancing with delight, like Thunder's. "You've made a new friend. How lovely."

Thunder looked even more thrilled when Lavender trotted up to Emily and whinnied with the biggest grin ever. "Hi, Emily," she said. "Good to meet you. Ivy has told me all about you. You sound great! I'd love to get to know you and Thunder better."

Emily smiled kindly and whispered to Ivy, "Aren't you the best friend ever? You already told Lavender about me!"

"Thanks," said Ivy. "We will be best friends forever!"

Emily thought of how lucky she was to be Ivy's friend. She turned to Thunder, who was telling Lavender how beautiful and grandiose he felt the Academy was.

"You're right! The Academy is wonderful. It's so grand. I looked at the map. There are so many places to explore, and I can't find just one place we can go to today!" Emily said. "But first, Thunds and I are going to the R—"

"Riding Arena!" Thunder finished with a thrilled

whinny. "I peeked at the map earlier. The arena looks amazing. It has hurdles and race paths and fields and what not! We can cross the rainforest to get there quickly," he added with a daring smile.

"Are you sure, Thunder? Ivy and I saw a sign that said that the rainforest is out of bounds," Emily protested.

"I'm sure. Come on, let's go! We'll be here till lunch if we don't hurry it up," Thunder exclaimed.

"But—" Ivy began.

"I promise you that it'll be safe," Thunder interrupted. "Let's go as fast as we can!" He reared up, hooves waving wildly in the air.

Emily ducked. "We'll see when we get there."

She climbed on Thunder and gestured to Ivy to get onto Lavender. Then she said to Ivy: "Let's trot to the Riding Arena. We will have to cross the path and—"

"Let's race instead," Thunder insisted. "Please,

Emily. I really want to! I've been in the stables the whole day, cooped up in that stall thing. I want to run."

"Sure…" Emily said slowly, getting onto Thunder. She was eager to race across the Academy. Even so, a part of her didn't feel so confident. She forced herself to grin. "Let's go!" she said shakily, trying not to think of the fast, bumpy race up ahead.

Could this ride get any scarier? Emily thought, gripping onto Thunder's mane so tight that her knuckles whitened.

Thunder whinnied in delight. "Lavender, the rock on the golden path is the start line!" he said. "Come on, or I'll start without you."

Emily's heart sped up. She wanted to tell Thunder not to race; she wasn't entirely sure if she wanted to canter on the first day. But she couldn't bring herself to speak up. She didn't want to disappoint Thunder. And to be honest, a part of her was excited.

But only a part of Emily was excited. The rest of her was really nervous.

Lavender and Thunder lined up with their riders on their backs. Ivy then decided, "I'll count!"

Emily, Thunder, and Lavender nodded.

"One," Ivy began as Thunder and Lavender struck the ground with their hooves, looking confident. "Two," Ivy said slowly while Emily told herself: It's okay. Thunder is super trustable! Come on, you have known him for a month already. No need to be afraid!

"Three! Go!" Ivy shouted and the horses immediately set off.

Thunder slammed his hooves on the ground and sprinted faster than the wind. Emily felt his legs pound and thunder on the ground every second.

"Go, Thunder, GO!" Emily urged. "You are the . . ." she paused as Thunder confidently jumped over a log ". . . best horse ever!" She clung onto Thunder's mane as he raced ahead of Lavender. But Lavender hadn't given up. She was getting faster and steadily catching up with Thunder.

"Come on, Lavender!" Ivy motivated her horse, who was panting and trying as hard as she could to catch up with Thunder. "You can do

this. You want to win, don't you? You can do it! Go, go, go!"

Emily shut her eyes as Thunder sprinted ahead. They were going at lightning speed, and she was afraid that she would fall off any second. Calming down for a second, she felt her horse's mane ripple in the wind as he went faster than Emily had seen anyone, or anything go in its life! Thunder was grinning from ear to ear as he pinched his eyes shut, too.

"Oh no!" neighed Lavender all of a sudden from behind, who had halted in her tracks. "Look Thunder! Up ahead!"

Emily snapped her eyes open to look at what Lavender was so worried about, her heart beating like a drum. It was a huge, fallen tree! It looked so dangerous. It had sharp branches that could scrape anyone, and there were bright red spiders everywhere on it. "Oh, my goodness!" Ivy breathed. "Those are poisonous Lava-Claw spiders! Isla told me about them! Their bite feels like fire, and they are burning hot." She looked worriedly at Thunder, who was struggling to stop in time. "Thunder! Halt!"

"Thunder!" Emily yelled. "Halt! Stop! Turn!" But it was too late. They were awfully close to the thorny, fallen tree infested with powerful Lava-Claw Spiders. "I can't, Emily!" Thunder panicked. "I'm too close to it. I was going too fast!"

Lavender stomped her hoof, looking worried. Jump it!" she whinnied. "Jump it! Jump it! Jump it!"

Emily hesitated. If there was one thing she hated, it was jumping high while riding a horse. She trembled. What if Thunder couldn't jump it? Would the spiders bite them? What if they barrelled into the tree?

"It's okay, Thunds! You're awesome!" shouted Emily. "And you're a genius. You'll jump over this log absolutely effortlessly."

Thunder neighed and Emily's heart skipped a beat. "One, two," Emily counted unsteadily. She hated jumping, and she wished that Thunder could have just halted sooner. She felt Thunder's muscles bunch as he bent down, ready to jump. "THREE!" He sprang like Emily had never seen him do before.

Chapter 5

Fun in the Forest!

"Yay, Thunder!" Ava cheered as Thunder soared high in the air. "Woohoo!"

A Lava-Claw spider spotted Emily and Thunder and started to leap. Emily bit back a groan. Things just kept getting worse! Just as Emily was convinced that they would be bitten by the most dangerous spider on the planet—and was

about to throw one of her shoes to scare it—Thunder landed. The Lava-Claw Spider scuttled away angrily and joined its group, feasting on some ants. There was a loud bang as Thunder's hooves thudded on the ground. Emily sighed in relief. She loved the way Thunder was so confident, but she still felt like avoiding riding.

She slid off Thunder and patted him. "Good, Thunder!" she told him, her voice trembling a little. "You jumped a huge, fallen tree! Should I get some fruit for you to have?" She brushed his forelocks out of his eyes, her legs still feeling like wobbly pineapple jelly.

Thunder nodded. "Okay. I am rather shaky after that tree jumping. I've honestly never done that before." He blushed. "But if you want to get me fruit, not sunbeam lemon or dragon fruit or winter nectarine. Never."

Emily giggled. She ran up to Ivy and asked, "Is there anything nutritious and edible in this rainforest? For horses? Like maybe some sort of fruit or berry or seed or feed or hay or oats or sweet or leaves or—"

"Emily, Thunder is fine, and I don't know," Ivy said, softly chuckling but trying to sound stern. "But I think I know who can tell us."

The next second, Emily and Ivy heard a strange, rustling sound. A tall oak tree bent forward and one of its branches hung loosely. It swayed in a sudden rush of air and broke off. The trees began to sway in the strong wind. Snap! Emily and Ivy sharply drew in their breath, afraid that some creature was lurking around. Emily's head whipped around, and she saw Thunder sitting with Lavender.

Ivy said in a low voice, "Isla, from our Crown, can help. She knew about the breed of Abby's cat. She has a nature and wildlife book. I also

saw flower seeds in her bag. Her bag toppled over a saddle and seeds tumbled out in the stables. I saw them and asked her what their names were. There were Blaze Blooms, Glitter Poppies, Pastel Petal Flowers, Lemon Blossoms, and River Coral Blooms. So, I think she knows a lot about vegetation. She must know what will give Thunder the energy he needs after such a gigantic leap."

She bit her lip as the rustling became louder. Emily ignored it but her heart was thundering against her chest.

"Yes, Isla would know." Emily forced herself to smile. "We need to find her. But that means riding back to the Crown." She paused to think. Her eyes darted to the swaying tree. Was it about to fall? She caught a sight of the colours of a flame—bright shades of yellow and orange. Was the tree going to catch fire? Oh no! Emily thought. She bit her lip as Ivy started talking.

"We need Isla. She said she would like to fly with Rocket, but I don't see her in the sky!" Ivy cried, glancing hopefully at the clouds overhead.

Suddenly, her eyes widened as the tree behind them shook and the rustling became a laugh.

"Then you should be glad I'm right here!" a voice exclaimed. A blonde girl on an orange pegasus came flying down. "It's me!" giggled Isla.

Ivy's eyes were full of shock. "How did you know we needed your help?" she demanded, bewildered. "How did you?"

Chapter 6

Finding the Riding Arena!

"Well," Isla explained, "I wanted to fly with Rocket, so we decided to trot to the Crown to tell our friends where we were going. Then we started to gallop on the golden path leading to the scary rainforest. When I was flying with Rocket, he saw a huge fallen tree and then I heard screaming and neighing. And then when I was about to tell Rocket that we should turn back, afraid there was trouble around, I heard a loud thump and more screaming." Isla enacted the scene on Rocket, making him do the screaming.

"I thought we should investigate," Rocket continued, "and then I saw you two, Ivy and Emily! You were talking about fruit that horses like, but I didn't want to interrupt."

"Then you brought me up in your conversation,"

Isla said, "and I heard you saying I could help you. So, well, I thought maybe I could surprise you because I *love, love, love* pranks! The end, you guys. Any questions?"

Ivy and Emily shook their heads, still shocked.

"Well, the fruits that you want are Lotus-Dew fruits. That patch, over there." Isla pointed to a small pond. Around it was bright green grass, and on it was a plant with a long stem with small shoots growing from it. At the end of each shoot, huge pink, orange, yellow, and purple fruits glimmered in the sunlight.

"Wow," marvelled Ivy, sitting down on some soft grass alongside Emily. "I wish I had my sketchpad to draw that pond!" She approached the pond slowly and stopped before the moss. "I think I see some fish, too."

Suddenly, a goose swam up to Ivy.

"Eek!" Ivy said in surprise. Startled, the goose flapped its wings and squawked loudly, calling her goslings.

Rocket flew past the goose, picked some fruit, and flung it to the other side of the pond. "Lotus-Dews are edible and taste really good," Isla told Emily. "My cousin's pony used to help me grow them back home for Rocket! Did you know that I have an entire greenhouse in the backyard of my home? I grow all sorts of plants there."

"Thunder, do you want to go pick a few fruits and share them around?" Emily asked her horse. "Oh, no, no," Ivy got up immediately. "I'll do it. You two are too kind!"

Lavender whinnied in agreement. "That's true," she added.

Ivy gestured to Lavender to go and get the Lotus-Dew fruit.

"Here's a basket, Lavender!" Isla enthusiastically handed a maroon basket to Ivy's pony.

Lavender treaded carefully to the edge of the mossy pond. She picked some of the fresh fruit, put a few in the basket and then gobbled up two herself. Once she was done eating, she passed the basket of fruits to Rocket and Thunder.

"Toss it in the air!" said Rocket, unfolding his wings and flapping them. Thunder helpfully picked a large purple-and-yellow fruit and flung it in the air. Rocket whooshed upwards and caught it swiftly in his mouth. "Mm, it's so good." He landed with a bump and munched on the fruit.

"It's good! Do you like it?" he asked Thunder. Thunder smiled and nodded. "Oh yes! It's delish!"

Once the ponies had finished half of the fruits in the basket, Emily waved bye-bye to Isla and Rocket. Turning to Thunder she said, "Come on, let's go to the Arena!"

Taking the basket from Lavender, Ivy also hopped onto Lavender.

Emily let Thunder finish his fruit, then held onto his mane tight, swung one leg across his side, and sat neatly on him.

"Let's go!" Emily called as Thunder started to trot along the path.

Soon the girls and their horses were deep in the rainforest. There were strange hoots, croaks, chirps, roars, water splashes, and hissing noises. Emily thought she heard a bush rustle behind her. Suddenly, a fox darted past them, making

Emily and Ivy jump. Emily decided she didn't want to stay in the rainforest for much longer. *What would be a fast way to get out of the rainforest?* As she was thinking, Emily saw another fallen tree on a patch of olive-green grass and remembered the adventure they had just had, from the stables to a race.

Wait, race . . . Emily smiled to herself. "Umm, how about we race?" she said. She really didn't want to race after the jumping in the rainforest, but she wanted Ivy and everyone else to be safe.

"That's a good idea," said Ivy at last. Emily nodded.

"Go!" exclaimed Ivy, clinging onto Lavender's mane as she galloped down the patch, the gravel kicking up behind her hooves.

"Can we go slow?" asked Emily tentatively. "Please?"

"And lose the race?" Thunder said, looking incredulous. "Emily, trust me."

"Okay, okay," sighed Emily.

She patted Thunder and took a deep breath, bracing herself for what was to come. "Let's go!" she cried as Thunder sped on the path in the rainforest.

Emily wobbled on Thunder's back and begged him to go slower.

"Emily, focus ahead of you and recite the riding tips I told you a week ago," he said firmly, cantering to the end.

"Fine, I guess," Emily groaned.

Heels down, back straight, head up, hold on, her mind chanted. *Heels down, back straight, head up, hold on!* When the crimson path ended, Lavender had won the race, thanks to her head start.

Thunder's hooves skidded as he halted, and Emily's face warmed in the sunlight as she rode out of the rainforest.

"Sorry, Thunds, but it seems like Lavender won," she murmured, bending forward and sliding off his back.

"Hmph," Thunder snorted in disbelief, though he sighed and trotted over to Lavender and congratulated her.

"Thunder!" Emily called out, deciding to tell him that she didn't want to ride anymore. Her horse came over to her. "I wanted to talk to you. I don't like—" Emily hesitated. Should she tell him her secret? No! Emily told herself. Keep it to yourself. *It'll hurt poor Thunder's feelings!* Emily put on her best fake grin as Thunder came over.

"You don't like what?" he asked.

"Um, I don't like . . . crimson," she invented, even though crimson was her favourite colour. "It's too . . . bright. I, um, wanted to tell you that because . . . some of the paths are crimson. This one was gold and crimson."

Thunder looked puzzled, "Okay . . . so you want me to paint over the path? Would blue be nice?"

Emily nervously shook her head and Thunder laughed.

"Come on, it is a short ride to the Arena," Ivy announced, showing up beside them. After five minutes of chatting about the Academy, the horses started to gallop. "Off to the Riding Arena!" sang Lavender, running beside Thunder.

As Thunder galloped across the path winding through a bunch of courts, Emily noticed fences around them and signs hanging on them. Emily read a few. On one side, she read the signs: Dog and Puppy Care, Puppy Meet-up Grounds, Cat Care, and Sense Court. Emily figured that the Sense Court would be a place for pets to practice their sniffing skills. She looked at the other side and gasped. *Even more signs!* Horse Vet, Puppy Vet, and Cat Vet!

After a while, Thunder and Lavender slowed down to a halt. "Here we are!" Lavender exclaimed.

"I can't wait to explore!" Thunder said.

"It looks even better than I imagined!" Ivy squealed.

The horses were trotting up to the entrance, when Emily spotted two girls with their dogs on leads. One girl had short, black hair and a friendly grin on her face. She was holding onto a purple lead that attached onto her puppy's harness. The girl was chatting with another girl, who had a long orange plait.

They both looked delighted.

The girl with short, black hair noticed the girls and their horses first, and waved. Her dog was drinking from a water bowl. It had the name "Rain" on it.

"Hey, Tisa," the girl with the orange plait said. "That's my dog's water bowl."

"Whoops!" said the other girl.

Emily decided that this was a fine time to say hello. "Hi there!" she said, waving at them.

"Hello," said the girl with the orange plait. "I'm Amber."

"Hey," the black-haired girl giggled. "Nice to meet you. My name's June, and this is my pup, Tisa."

Tisa woofed happily, her long lashes fluttering in the breeze. She cheekily pawed her owner's purse. "Okay! One more treat and then we take a five-hour break, cool?" June let her puppy fish inside her purse and crack open the treat box.

"We were just about to head into the arena," June continued. Tisa woofed again and rolled over on the grass.

"June's right," she said, giggling. "I hope there's stuff for pups to do in the Arena too. I hope it's not too . . . *horse-y*."

Tisa daintily walked up to Ivy and Emily and whispered, "I'm so much fun, and I'm a puppy," she grinned, "but, is it boring to have a horse? They seem too tall to play fetch, and they can't wag, and they don't eat pumpkin treats, and they don't have paws. And, wait, can they even *fit* into hollow strawberry-shaped pillows?"

Tisa's voice got louder as she whispered, and soon everyone could hear her. They all burst out laughing. Emily noticed that Thunder's eyes held a mischievous twinkle.

Chapter 7

Games and Pets

June smiled apologetically at the girls. "Tisa's very honest!" she whispered. "I, um, hope she didn't offend your ponies."

Emily shook her head. "My horse is quite good-natured."

"Mine too," said Ivy.

Emily smiled as Lavender galloped over to Tisa. "We don't fit in strawberry pillows, Tisa, but can pups whicker?" Lavender smirked, hiding her laugh.

Emily heaved a sigh of relief, glad that Lavender had taken Tisa's words with a smile.

"Can puppies gallop? Oh, and can puppies neigh?" Thunder asked, coming over to Lavender.

"Good one," Tisa replied, her eyes glinting. "Show me what you can do."

Thunder's eyes sparkled as he ran full speed in a circle and then fearlessly leapt a fence. He jumped back into the arena and landed on his hind legs. Tisa gasped. "Wow!" she said, admiring Thunder's agility. "You're better at tricks than I am! But I think I do the 'Be a Dog' trick better than you," she joked.

"Well, check *this* out!" Thunder twirled on his hind legs and then tried to balance on one hoof. Emily watched eagerly. She thought he looked like an elegant ballerina.

Thump! . . . Or maybe flat pancake.

Everyone giggled. "At least now I know I'm heavier than a mouse!" Thunder said as he stood up. Then, he nuzzled Emily and asked, "Did you like my trick?"

Emily gave him a smile. "Of course. You're the best horse ever." She wrapped her arms tightly around Thunder. "You're so talented. Do you want some water?"

Thunder shook his head. "I'm good, thanks."

But Emily wasn't listening. She found a drinking trough and ushered Thunder to it. Thunder was busy talking with Tisa and Lavender, but he trotted up to Emily gratefully. He lowered his head and began to drink. A grey toy poodle was walking nearby. It had a crystal collar displaying a faded name.

"Who is this?" Lavender asked politely, looking at the poodle. Emily tried to read the name but could only make out two letters: R and N. The dog's black eyes held a haughty look. Thunder flicked his mane and tail and frowned. "I don't like him much," he muttered to Emily and Ivy. "And that's saying a lot because we haven't even met him yet."

"That's Rain," sighed June. Her face fell. "Rain and Tisa aren't friends. Rain belongs to Amber, the girl I was talking with a while ago."

How can anyone not like Tisa? She is cool. I'd love to have someone like Tisa as a pet. "Tisa is amazing," Emily said to comfort June.

June's face brightened again.

She bent to the ground and told Tisa, "You hear that? You are amazing. Everyone thinks so!"

Tisa cheered up after being told this. "So, maybe . . ." She looked at June's handbag, pawing at it so its pink glitter sprinkled off it.

"Fine, fine!" June rolled her eyes and laughed. She opened her handbag and gave Tisa a treat. Giving Tisa a light kiss on her fringe, June zipped her colourful bag up again.

Emily noticed that the poodle was stomping closer to them. "Why hello there, Rain!" Ivy said cheerfully to the grey toy poodle. "Why aren't you and your friend in the Arena?" she asked.

Rain snorted. "Tisa isn't my friend!" he scowled. "I don't like her. I don't know why a Shih Tzu would *continuously* want to be friends with me, me who is a superior poodle!" He lifted his head high.

"More like *arrogant* poodle," Thunder muttered under his breath.

Rain didn't hear Thunder. "You know what else? Amber's mom watched a documentary about animals . . ." Rain paused dramatically, "and it said that Shih Tzus are *dogs*!" he exclaimed in disgust. "At least I'm a poodle and not a *dog*!"

"You know, poodles are dogs too," Tisa chipped in, looking annoyed.

Emily bit her lip, stuck in the middle of the two puppies arguing. Tisa leapt closer to Rain and snarled. Rain stuck his nose up in the air. Smirking, he told the others, "Listen, I am happily lying down, and Tisa comes up to me, sniffs me and wakes me up—"

"And he barks at me and tries to shoo me away!" Tisa exclaimed, sounding irked, despite her cheerful tone.

Rain added, "And then she walks away, leaving me awake." He looked around. "It's just so unpleasant to be around others," he continued. "Waking me up . . . petting me . . . changing my collar . . . oh, and those *mice* who always eat my tuna soup mix!" he scowled, and June and Ivy raised their eyebrows.

"Yeah, okay, but why aren't you and *Tisa* in the Arena?" asked Ivy, making sure that she didn't say the word "friend".

"Oh, yes, it's the *Riding* Arena you know, we don't gallop, us poodles. Can't you see that I am shorter than an actual horse?" Rain laughed rudely, ignoring everyone's incredulous stares. "Probably *not*!"

"Rain!" Amber, the girl with the orange plait, said firmly but calmly. "You may not like Tisa, but you can't be so nasty with her. I may as well report you to Starlight, the principal unicorn, Feather, the principal puppy, Silky, the principal cat, or Angel, the principal Pegasus. If you don't behave, I have a feeling that they will send you to the *detention room*. If you refuse to stay there—well, I don't know what we shall do! Please say sorry, acknowledge others' feelings, think before you speak, and realize that Ivy—"

"No, no. Rain, you shouldn't have done what you did but just make sure you don't do it again," Ivy explained gently.

Rain looked tense.

"Maybe you should apologize," Emily suggested kindly.

Rain looked apologetic. "Hmph. Sorry," he growled, and even managed a small smile.

"It's okay," Ivy said to Rain and Amber. She grinned at Rain and bent down to softly pat him. Rain's eyes flashed and it seemed like he was about to bite when he caught the look in Amber's eyes. He didn't move as Ivy continued to pet him.

"I realize I haven't introduced myself. I'm Ivy, though you probably already know that. And my horse is Lavender."

Amber nodded. "Sure. She's the palomino, yes?"
"Exactly," said Ivy. "Rain, how about you go hang out with your f—"

Amber's hand flew to Ivy's mouth. "Don't say 'friend'! He'll get steamed up again because, well, he doesn't want friends so he would not want for anyone to assume he has some," she hissed.

Ivy nodded. "Um, I mean, the *others*."

Rain walked over to Tisa, who was standing near June, and said, "Well, since you upset me, you'll need to clean the stables for seven years. Council's orders."

"You're not even in the School Council," Tisa said, raising an eyebrow.

Rain laughed. "Cleaning the stable order isn't *my* rule," he lied.

Tisa raised the other eyebrow.

"Um, well, maybe it is," admitted Rain.

Tisa shrugged. "I knew it. I knew that, and I also know that you've hidden one of June's mint biscuits behind your collar." She shot Rain a hostile glare and sauntered on.

Emily frowned as Rain shook his collar and a cookie fell out. *It looks like Rain just doesn't know how to be around others. If he behaved, he'd make friends in no time. And he'd also stop stealing mint cookies.*

Emily grinned and told June what she thought. "I guess I'd be able to keep my biscuits if we tried it," June said with a giggle. "Just kidding. Let's try it." She high-fived Emily and told Tisa her plan. Tisa nodded slowly as her owner talked to her, and then her eyes widened with understanding. "Righty-o, Captain June!" She stole another doggy treat before June could react, and then walked up to Rain.

"For you!" Tisa said, smiling. She dropped the biscuit at Rain's paws. "I hope you like it."

Rain looked at it with wide eyes, forgetting his annoyance. "Th-thank you," he said, looking a little astonished at Tisa's generosity. He took a bite and swallowed. "That's, well, pretty generous. What . . . what flavour is this?"

Tisa grinned. "You like it, don't you?"

Chapter 8
New Friends

Tisa curled up with Rain and answered, "Um, it's chicken, blueberry, and cottage cheese. Obviously." She smacked her lips and took a bite.

"You seem to like it," Rain pointed out, looking at Tisa, who was gazing at the biscuit.

"I do. It's the only thing that gets me to roll over," Tisa said.

Rain smirked, his eyes flashing with playfulness. He ran to a bush and picked up a fallen leaf from the plant nearby. He held it in his mouth and tickled Tisa until she rolled over and laughed and laughed. "See? Even I can make you roll over. Behold Rain, the Poodle Who is Almost as Powerful as a Dog Treat!"

"Stop!" Tisa chuckled. "You should work at the Pet Spa for a while. This tickle feels good!" She hooted with laughter.

"Mm . . ." Rain glanced towards the biscuit.

"You know, I'd rather eat the whole afternoon; I bet I'll love this flavour. It must taste heavenly. Cottage cheese . . . blueberry . . . chicken . . ."

Emily, Thunder, Ivy, Amber, Lavender, and June grimaced. Seeing the others' faces, Tisa said, "Come on! June, you love blueberry."

"And Amber, your mom loves chicken," Rain reminded his owner.

"Yeah, and I like both," Ivy told him. "But not *combined*."

"I like blueberries, too," Lavender neighed. "Once I had a full crate of them and my mouth turned blue!" She blushed. "And I love cheese too, but I've never *eaten* it before." Lavender became redder. "And what's a cottage?"

Emily smiled. "A house."

Lavender looked confused. "House cheese? That sounds strange!"

Everyone chuckled. "You'd enjoy cooking lessons," Ivy teased.

"Come on, let's feast," Tisa told Rain, looking happy to sit down with him and share the treat with him.

The pups giggled as they chatted, and then Rain whispered to Tisa, "From now on, I think I'll like you a little, because you've, um, proved you're a friend I can trust. I'm honestly sorry that I was mean to you earlier, but I just did that because I used to live my own life and think my own thoughts back in Amber's home, and I was kind of the 'pampered pet' there. But even though letting me make new friends wasn't the reason I'm here today, I'm sort of glad I have." He paused. "Also, though we're friends now, please have other pals too. Because, you know, I still don't want to be around pups *all* the time."

Emily chuckled, deciding that Rain mustn't want a companion who was by his side twenty-four seven.

Tisa and June glanced at Rain. "Yes, I'm a bit

picky about which dogs I like," Tisa admitted.

"Well, okay, let's explore the Arena," said Ivy, grinning. "It's about time!"

Emily nodded. Now was a good time to do what they needed to!

"Come on, pups!" Lavender said, looking quite ecstatic. "Let's go to the Riding Arena!"

Rain looked confused. "But we aren't horses!" he insisted, puzzled. Then Tisa whispered to Rain, loud enough for the girls to hear: "I think it's only the Riding Arena when the riding classes are taking place . . ."

"Otherwise, I guess it's just the *Arena*!" Rain finished, seeming much friendlier. He nodded and said, "That is a good theory, Tisa. It makes sense."

"It's true," Ivy said. "Ms. Smith, the riding teacher, told us that."

Lavender said, "Smart Tisa! That's right," and

gave Tisa a Lotus-Dew fruit, tired of holding the basket in her mouth. Rain smiled and laughed as Tisa had a bite of the purple, yellow, orange, and pink fruit, that was approximately the size of a glow-daisy. Emily knew that because she loved daisies. Then, Rain got up and walked to the gate with Tisa.

They both pawed the white brick gate until Tisa's face lit up. "I just got an idea!" she said in excitement. Her eyes twinkled. "We can climb up the gate."

Rain gaped. "Do we . . . have to?"

"Oh Rain, you look uncertain. You can just ride Thunder." Tisa didn't waste another second. She jumped high near the middle of the gate. She landed on one of the white bricks that jutted out from the gate, stood on her hind legs, and jumped again, landing smoothly on top of the gate.

With complete confidence, she jumped down, now inside the arena. Then came a muffled voice that Emily recognized as Tisa: "Come on,

Rain!" Rain nodded. "Let me get on your back along with Amber," he demanded to Thunder.

Amber looked surprised but happily got onto Thunder's back with her poodle in her arms. "I can try!" she said positively. Thunder swiftly jumped over the white gate and landed effortlessly on the other side.

Ivy nodded expectantly at Emily. Emily smiled, but before pushing the door open, she called: "Stand clear of the gate, pups, and horse!"

She pushed the gate open and gasped as Lavender trotted in and jumped around. The Riding Arena was huge! It had two circle-shaped riding paths,

hurdles, plain grass, and many trees. It was perfect.

But it's perfect in the wrong way. A well-built arena for jumping and galloping? No way! Thunder will fall in love with it, and he'll want to come here daily. How do I tell him I dislike riding now?

"I *cannot* wait to explore!" Thunder and Lavender said at the same time. They sure were excited. Emily looked at them and put her hands on her hips. *Well, I can wait!*

As the girls and their horses explored the Arena, they saw a group of three girls and their pets. Two were horses and one was a unicorn. She was bright lime in colour and had glittery shooting stars patterned all over her. On her flank, a sparkly monstera leaf stood out. Her rider, a girl with chocolate-brown hair tied in two amazingly short ponytails, waved at them. "Hi there, girls!" she called out.

"Hola!" the unicorn said in Spanish, nuzzling her owner's bright red dress.

Sensing that the girl and her unicorn were friendly, the group made their way to them. "Hello," said the girl. "My name is Jessica." She patted her unicorn. "And this is Sparkle."

Sparkle reared up and whinnied, "Yep, that's me!"

Thunder stared at Sparkle, wide-eyed. "Can you do magic?" he asked.

"What do you think this is for?" Sparkle asked with a chuckle, pointing at her horn. "Magic. Of course, I can do some."

Jessica hurried to her unicorn's side and said anxiously. "Sparkle, you are a beginner. I don't think you should try magic before your lessons. I don't want you to turn a tree into a crocodile or something."

Sparkle held her head high, taking Jessica's words with a smile. "That's true. But, well, there is no harm in trying, is there, Jessica?"

Jessica's eyes twinkled. "Well, I suppose there

isn't. Okay. You can try," she said confidently. "I believe in you."

Sparkle leapt in the air and shook her forelocks out of her eyes. "Presenting . . ." she said theatrically, swishing her mane and giving a bow, ". . . the Frosty Confetti Dance! I've seen my cousin, Monarch, do it. Whenever she does it, the swirly rainbows that shoot out of her horn take shapes of an object you're thinking of, but I've not learnt how to do that yet."

"It sounds awesome!" Emily said.

Sparkle whinnied, galloping in a circle. She lowered her horn and pointed it right above the group. "Prepare to be amazed!"

Green, navy blue, and golden light swirled in the sky. A pastel blue cloud formed, and as it parted, snowflakes fell everywhere. Ribbons of light danced above the girls and pets. Everyone gasped. This was so awesome!

The strips of light twirled about and faded. Sparkle shot an apologetic smile at everyone watching. "Sorry, I haven't learnt how to keep the light in the sky for long yet. But I bet I will once lessons start!" Everyone chorused, "It's okay! You were brilliant!"

"But—" Rain began.

The pets cheered even though Emily noticed that Rain was about to argue about the lights.

"What about . . ." Sparkle wondered. "I can do another piece of magic for you. I can do *Butterfly and Sunshine* for you. It's amazing. The sun shines so bright in this act, and you'll feel like you're floating on a rainbow." Emily, Jessica, Tisa, Amber, Ivy, and June nodded while Rain said, "Make sure we don't get sunburned!"

Sparkle pointed her horn towards an apple tree and the leaves started to float towards her. They started to take shape of . . . "Butterflies!" Tisa marvelled.

Sparkle nodded, concentrating. "Exactly."

She was panting a little. Suddenly, a burst of light flew out from her horn and the tree leaves took full shape of butterflies.

They fluttered their purple and yellow wings, and glided over to Sparkle. They doubled in quantity every few seconds, forming a butterfly dome above everyone. Emily heard some cheers from the other side of the Arena but could not see who was cheering, as the butterflies were blocking her view.

Sparkle's eyes shone bright as she galloped through the butterflies. She angled her horn towards the sun. In a second, its rays were as bright as summer. The butterflies took the shapes of letters. Soon they spelled out, *Sunshine!*

Emily watched the spectacle, her mouth agape.

Sparkle sprinted through the pack of butterflies, rainbow colours swirling in her eyes.

"What's going on?" a strict voice boomed in the Arena. "Why are there butterflies everywhere? And I hope these are not Marble-Glass butterflies. Their wings leave off marble dust that is dangerous for puppies. And I'm sure I saw a dog around here somewhere. Was it you, Tisa?" Sparkle panicked and the butterflies faded and blew away.

"Who made those?" the voice questioned sternly. "If those are Marble-Glass butterflies then you are causing a lot of harm for the dogs around here." An off-white cat—a little smaller than a leopard—appeared. She was walking in Sparkle's direction.

"Oh no!" Thunder whispered. "That's Silky, the principal cat! Don't let her catch you!"

"It's okay!" Sparkle assured everyone.

Silky reached the group, looking here and there in confusion. Emily closed her eyes in panic, trying to think of a place to hide. She expected Sparkle to get a firm scolding, but all she heard was, "Huh? I was sure those were created by magic. Well, it's alright." She walked away.

"I made us invisible," Sparkle explained, panting. "It was hard work, but Principal Silky would get cross otherwise. She's nice, but very sharp. Her meow-shouts are also too loud. She hisses loudly, too, but thankfully never scratches."

Sparkle looked over her shoulder to where Tisa

was brushing herself frantically. "Um, Tisa, Rain, don't worry. Those were enchanted fir tree butterflies, not Marble Glass ones. I mean, come on! Why would I try to harm you all?" She giggled at Tisa, who was *still* rubbing her skin with all her might.

"Tisa, those were *not* harmful!" she said loudly. Tisa shook herself one more time and then sat down for another treat.

Just then, a girl with black eyes and sparkling gold shoes came over to them. She was clearly very shy, but plucked up the courage to speak. "Hi. I'm Teresa."

Emily waved at Teresa welcomingly. "My name's Emily. This is my best friend, Ivy, and my horse, Thunder."

Chapter 9
The Secret Journey

Jessica got off Sparkle and walked over to Teresa and Emily. "Teresa, June, Amber, Kate, Jennifer, and I are all in the same Crown, Magic Crown. Emily, Ivy, I would love to visit yours sometime soon! We can be Crown buddies. Speaking of which . . ." Jessica stopped and looked around.

"It's been lovely meeting you all, honest. But we've been in the Riding Arena for an hour now, and I think we should go to our Diamonds now. I can't wait to see mine!"

"Sure. We'll catch up later," winked Ivy.

Jessica called to her friends, "Come on! Let's go. I bet our other friends are in their Diamonds."

Sparkle stood beside Jessica and frowned at the mention of all the people going to their rooms.

"I don't like the stables," she announced. "Jess, is it okay if I stay here?"

"Of course, Sparks," said Jessica warmly, stroking her unicorn's lime green mane.

"Wonderful!" said Thunder, delighted. "I don't like the stables either, you know."

After some time, Thunder suggested they play a game. "Races, hurdles, tag, hide and seek, or any other games you like."

Barely waiting for Thunder to finish, everyone chorused, *"Races or tag!"*

Emily hesitated. "Um, are we going to sit on our horses for the race?" she asked.

Thunder looked incredulous. "I've never heard of a horse race that had the rider sitting on a chair. But we could play tag first."

Emily breathed a huge sigh of relief.

Once Ivy got onto Lavender, Emily onto Thunder,

and Sparkle on her own, the game started. Sparkle decided she would be "it".

"One . . . two . . ." Sparkle began counting, "three!"

The game had started! Before Emily could say anything, Thunder took off at lightning speed. Surprisingly, Sparkle could run nearly as fast as him. "I almost got you!" Sparkle exclaimed, her fluorescent, lime green mane and tail rippling in the breeze.

"Um, Thunder, um . . ." Emily wanted to tell Thunder to slow down, but he was focusing on speeding ahead, so he mistook "um" for "run". Emily thought it impossible that Thunder could go any faster, but he did. He sped up even more. "Thunder!" Emily's tummy churned. She clung onto Thunder's mane as tight as possible, bouncing like jelly on his back.

The game continued. Eventually, Sparkle fell behind Thunder, unable to match his speed. He turned on his heels and began to chase Ivy, but she and her pony couldn't go on. "We want a break!" Ivy said. "We're too tired!"

Emily shot a grateful look to Ivy. "Yes! Me, too. Maybe we should take a break and chat." Emily waited for Thunder to say something. To her immense relief, Thunder nodded and said, "Good idea."

Emily felt ten tons lighter! Her mind relaxed, and she thought of other things. As she started talking, she couldn't stop. "In environmental studies, I really hope we learn about the rainforest. It was so frightening when we passed through it, though. For me at least." She looked around the arena. "There must be all sorts of fascinating areas in Animal Academy. Like the magic court where unicorns practise magic. Even the vets sound exciting! I'd love to see baby animals with them. Like a baby sloth! Ooh, or maybe a baby lemur? I dream of becoming a vet myself, you know."

Ivy raised an eyebrow. "Really? I thought you were into cooking," she said.

Emily nodded. "Oh, right! I am. It's so confusing to decide what you want to be. Maybe I want to be a vet-chef?"

"That probably is a thing," winked Thunder.

"Oh! This reminds me! When we eat lunch, I'll go to the horse-field and serve Thunder first," Emily went on. "Pets first! Do you think we'll bake something for our pets during cooking lessons?"

"Whoa! Slow down!" Thunder said with a huge smile on his face. "I hope we get to solve a mystery or go on an adventure. Imagine us solving—" Thunder was interrupted by a horse's loud whinny.

It was a unicorn. She was light, flamingo-pink with (Emily counted) twenty-eight small golden stars all over her. Her horn glowed a fabulous colour of orange-pink.

"Good afternoon, everyone," she said, swishing her silver mane and tail. The unicorn announced, "I'm the head unicorn, Starlight Silverwave. Please, all people, go to the feeding field on the map and serve your horses as per their liking. You must be there by half past noon. After they finish, ride them to the cafeteria. The dogs will go to the puppy section of the café and cats to their section. Cat and dog food will be in the pet section of the café. You will all have an Animal Academy rule booklet in every Diamond of the Crowns."

Emily nodded. She knew what Diamonds were. They were your very own section of a Crown. They were small sections with walls and a door to go into your neighbour's Diamond. Emily believed Rainbow Crown's Diamonds' walls were rainbow-coloured or patterned with rainbows.

Emily ran to Thunder and climbed onto him. She clutched his mane to keep herself steady as he galloped. "Thunder, do you know where the cafeteria is?" Emily asked.

Thunder flicked his tail and his ears twitched.

"Yes," he said carefully, making sure that he was giving Emily correct directions. "It's at the far end of the Academy. The only way to reach there in time is to go at lightning speed." Thunder swished his tail again. "If we don't want to, then . . . I have another plan!" Thunder's eyes sparkled. Emily's heart fluttered, with both excitement and fear. She was delighted that they weren't going to go at lightning speed, but, knowing Thunder, she knew they were going to do *something* daring.

"Alright," she said, her wavy ponytail flying in the breeze. "Let's go!"

Thunder now galloped even faster. He galloped past the hurdles, ignored the inviting race path and then . . . Emily grew anxious and afraid as Thunder prepared to jump the fence!

Emily shut her eyes tightly. A few long seconds passed. When Emily opened her eyes next, she was on the other side of the fence. *I don't believe it*! she thought. Thunder had made such a high jump and she had breezed through it. "Nice jump," Emily said, patting her horse.

"Thanks." Thunder slowed his pace now and eventually came to a stop at a fenced area with a tiny grotto at one side. Emily climbed off him. "This way. Follow me," Thunder directed.

As Emily walked on the fresh, turquoise grass, she spotted patches of Sugar Bell Blooms. She found a watering can and watered them a little, because to her, they looked a little pale. She turned and noticed feeding bins. Some bins were piled high with hay, others with multicoloured leaves and the last ones with fruits, Lotus-Dew leaves, fresh blossoms, round berries, and oats.

Horses were eating from the troughs.

"This is the Horse Feeding Field!" Emily exclaimed, looking around. She then decided to feed Thunder. First, he ate the hay, then Lotus-Dew leaves, Lemon Blossoms, and then Blaze Blooms.

"Eat up!" Emily said kindly. He looks adorable, she thought as Thunder began to chew. She closed her eyes, hearing the cheerful sound of bluebirds and parakeets singing together.

"Emily, hurry! You need to follow me into the cottage to get to the cafeteria on time," Thunder said after five minutes, finishing the last cherry. "Or do you want to get into trouble with Starlight?"

Emily froze. Starlight Silverwave *did* look like she demanded perfection. "Whoops! I almost forgot that *I* have to eat!"

Emily followed Thunder into an old cottage at the side of the Horse Feeding Field. "What is this?" she breathed.

"It used to be a library, but now I think it's just a storeroom," Thunder replied. He bent down near a bookshelf. He nudged past book after book. After a minute, he paused at a book titled *The Terplantatious,* and pulled a lever. Suddenly, there was a creak and a huge tunnel appeared before them. A secret passageway! Emily thought, excited. It was big enough to fit something double the size of Thunder, so going in it would be a breeze, too!

"Climb in!" urged Thunder. Emily entered the tunnel. She appeared calm, but inside, her heart was beating faster than Thunder's gallops! "How do you know about this, Thunder?" she asked.

Thunder shook his forelocks out of his eyes. "I used to be part of a herd when I was young, and I had briefly known this foal called Onyx. Later he found a girl called Rebecca and they really bonded with each other." He smiled.

"And? How did this lead to the discovery of the tunnel?" asked Emily, itching to go further into the tunnel.

"Soon Onyx left the herd and joined Rebecca here, at Animal Academy," Thunder told her.

"And . . .?

"Later, I left the herd, longing for an adventure and a new friend. My mum stayed with me for a short time before becoming a well-known racehorse, and my dad found a rider and started learning dressage. A year after moving to Sunshine Meadows on my own, and only a week before I met you, I stumbled upon one of my old foalhood friends who was leaving for Animal Academy with a girl called Ana. He said we could keep in touch and be pen pals."

"Please get to your point!" Emily begged.

"Just two days ago, I received a letter from him saying that he had found a secret tunnel while playing hide-and-seek. I wrote back, telling him that I was about to join the school and would check it out."

Emily's eyes shimmered. "That's such a nice story," she said softly. From what Thunder had just told her, she'd learnt a lot about his life.

She realized how resilient and courageous he had been, leaving his herd. And what warmed her most was that he had left his home for *his* happiness.

She thought about how Thunder had left his herd because he longed for new adventures and new friends.

He wanted to find new friends not because he had a fight with one, or that one moved away, like Onyx. He wanted more friends because he knew everyone in his herd. And, I like the reason he moved away too! I love my family so much, but if I were to stay with Mum and Dad for my whole life, it would get so boring!

Just like Thunder, I have moved away from home. I've come to Animal Academy. Can't wait to begin my new life full of adventures, Emily thought, smiling.

Emily's stomach rumbled. She figured what was

important was to go fast in the passageway. So, Emily began to run. She liked many sports, like basketball, racquetball, mini golf, and badminton, and was now beginning to think that she didn't mind running either.

Thunder paced behind Emily, careful not to step on her by accident or slip on one of the sharp rocks that fell from the top of the tunnel every few seconds.

After five minutes of sprinting, the passage became steep. "Slide time!" said Thunder happily. Emily sat down on the steep slope and started to slide down. She cheered as she reached the end of the slide.

"I'm down now, Thunds. You can start to slide!" Emily said. She got up in a hurry, moving a fair distance away from where she had landed. She glanced at the next bit of the tunnel. It was narrower and shorter and had a floor of soil. She walked forward and into the tunnel, realizing it looked more like a maze now that she was in it. There were four forks—one going right, one straight, one straight and then left, and one left. After thinking for a few seconds, Emily chose the third one.

Suddenly she heard a loud thump, louder than any sound Thunder can make simply getting off the steep slope. She was worried now. What if Thunder, in his excitement, had reared up at the thought of sliding, then lost his balance at the edge of the slope and tumbled down? If so, was he alright? Emily had already made her way into the third fork so she could not see him. She instantly turned and ran to the end.

Thunder looked afraid. He slowly got up.

"Was it you?" Emily demanded breathlessly. "Did you make the noise? Did you fall down?" Thunder looked at her for a few seconds, and then looked up at the ceiling. "Shh!" he hissed. "It was something overhead. Let's go quietly so we don't get discovered."

Emily's heart fluttered in relief. "It was probably an animal, as this tunnel goes through the rainforest. Now, let's go! It's been way too long; you need to eat!"

Emily felt light as a feather upon hearing Thunder. As she walked ahead with Thunder, she spotted a rectangular piece of wood in the ceiling. "What is that?" she wondered aloud.

Thunder swished his mane. "I'm not sure, but I think you can get in from the rainforest using that."

Emily nodded. She got onto Thunder, and they galloped through the tunnel. After two minutes, Thunder announced, "The passage is turning upwards." He was right! It suddenly looked like a rock-climbing frame, except with fewer yet larger footholds. "I'll jump up to get onto the next foothold, so hold onto me tightly."

Emily did as she was told. No way she would fall off him!

As Emily and Thunder got out of the tunnel, they realized that they were by the library door. "Okay, Thunder, you can go back to the stables. I think I gave you a big lunch, so how about you use that energy to gallop the whole way back without the tunnel?" Emily said, winking.

"Nice try," giggled Thunder. "Have a good lunch!" He turned away and pranced to the tunnel, when his ears pricked up and he joked, "Bring me back dessert!"

"Bye!" waved Emily.

She strode into the cafeteria. She was amongst the first to arrive, thanks to the secret passage. I will use it every day! Emily decided. It was all working out. She began to form her daily routine in her mind. Thunder will eat his meal at around noon, and then they can go in the passage and be early for her lunch, resulting in extra time to go somewhere before lessons resume.

"Wow; I've never seen a cafeteria so huge!" Emily marvelled, gazing in awe at the large buffet. She served herself a bowl of tomato soup, pasta with cheese sprinkled on top, and some hot rolls with red and green bell pepper and cottage cheese inside. Magic Crown's table was next to Rainbow Crown's, and Emily noticed that Jessica was piling seven rolls high on her plate!

The hour of lunch flew and soon after, the cooks and students who had offered to help, brought out dessert. Emily gasped in wonder. So many desserts! Emily had never seen such splendid desserts ever in her life—mini chocolate cupcakes with strawberry and pineapple icing, heart-shaped cookies with raspberries and coconut, and various fruit milkshakes topped with whipped cream and chocolate flakes. Even though every single person in the cafeteria wanted to have the cupcakes, milkshakes, and cookies, they still knew that one was best, as you don't want to be too full to ride or play with your pets.

Emily went up to the milkshake stand and chose the most delicious-looking one. It had vanilla sprinkles atop the coconut and mango whipped cream. A short cook with black hair and a kind smile spoke gently to Emily, Abby, Isla, and Jessica. She said, "I guarantee that none of the cherries have seeds in them. Bon appétit!"

Isla licked her lips. "Are the cherries grown in the North Emerald Grasslands? The weather conditions over there are ideal for cherries and it is a vast grassland, too."

The cook looked impressed. "Wow, you're the smart one! These cherries are grown there."

Chapter 10
Kittens and More Friends!

June, who was passing by the milkshake stand, joked, "Isla, do you mean the Emerald *Glass* lands?" Isla, and the others within earshot, burst out laughing.

"Good one, June!" Abby giggled.

Amber, sitting next to Jessica, laughed with her, saying, "Jess, Emeralds! Glass!"

Jessica nodded while sipping her milkshake. "Yep! Well, wherever the cherries are from, they're yummy!" She gobbled her cherry up.

As Emily drank her milkshake, she spotted several girls come in, talking nonstop. One girl who was giggling and talking with her friends waved to Emily. She had long, wavy, golden hair and cheerful light-blue eyes that twinkled.

She was wearing a knee-length turquoise dress and glittery white shoes. "Hello!" she said. "I am River and I'm here with my friends. We are all getting food for our pets. My cat's name is Darling Baby Li Li."

Emily tilted her head slightly. "Really?" she asked, stifling a giggle. *Imagine a cat called Darling Baby Li Li!*

River blushed. "Um, not really. His name is Leo!"

"Aww, Leo sounds so cute. Is he a mixed breed?"

River shook her head. "No, he is a British Bi-Colour Shorthair. My best friend Lisa now owns his mum, Xena. I owned Xena first, but since the Academy's rule is that you can only have one pet, I gave Xena to Lisa. I'm so glad they like each other!"

June and Amber joined Emily.

"Yep, Leo sounds adorable!" Amber agreed.

June pushed her short, black hair behind her

shoulders. "Yes, I agree with Amber. Leo's breed must be awesome. But did you know all the dog breeds are the cutest ones ever? There are Cavachons, Morkies, Shorkies, Cockapoos, and Goldendoodles! There are also breeds that are not mixed, like Shih Tzus, Jack Russel Terriers, and toy poodles."

Amber smiled. "I have a toy poodle. His name is Rain. He is friends with June's dog. What are Cavachons, Morkies, Shorkies, Goldendoodles, and Cockapoos?"

Emily wondered the same.

June greeted a girl with light brown hair who came in. She was wearing a light lilac top with a black and white cat printed on it and her skirt was made of layers of light blue lace. "Hi," she said cheerfully.

"Hello! My name is Lisa. What's yours?" said the girl, grinning from ear to ear.

"June," said June, beaming back.

Letting Lisa into the conversation she was having, June told everyone, "All of those breeds: Cavachons, Morkies, Shorkies, Goldendoodles, and Cockapoos, are mixed breeds. Cockapoos are Cocker Spaniels and poodles."

The girls nodded.

"Goldendoodles are poodles and golden retrievers. Cavachons are a mix between the Cavalier King Charles Spaniel and the Bichon Frise breeds," continued June. "Morkies are Maltese and Yorkshire Terrier crossbreeds, and Shorkies are one of my favourites because they are a cross between a Shih Tzu and a Yorkshire Terrier."

June giggled. "My dog is a Shih Tzu called Tisa. She's literally as cute as all these breeds combined!"

"June isn't lying; Tisa really is!" Emily agreed. "I've met her."

"That sounds nice. My cat's name is Xena and

she's really pretty," said Lisa. "She's *so* elegant."

Just then, a girl wearing a purple striped dress with a green dinosaur on it, said, "My puppy's name is Tulip, and she is an adorable Morkie. A cross between a Maltese and a Yorkshire Terrier. Oh, and my name is Ella."

A girl with dark red hair and hazel eyes pushed past Ella. "I'm Scarlet and I have a Cockapoo. Speaking of which, why are we all standing around here? Our pups will starve!"

As the group filed away, Emily kept her empty milkshake glass on the counter and hurried to the *enter/exit* door, pushing it open. She heard

a voice like Victoria's, calling, "Emily, where are you going?"

Emily just replied, "Nowhere, really. Um, just to the Diamonds."

And before Victoria could say anything more, she ran towards the library and got into the passage. She sprinted and ended up in the cottage. She saw the book again titled *The Terplantatious.* The compact book had an image of a big turtle with an orange shell and a gleaming pearl-white body. She picked it up and shoved it into her watermelon-pink pocket.

After some time, Emily reached the stables. She searched for Thunder's nameplate. Soon, she found it and patted her horse's head. "What were you doing all this time?" she asked.

Thunder looked happy to see Emily. "Oh, nothing really. Just eating hay and chatting with my neighbours, Lotus, and Amethyst."

"Are you getting to know them well?"

Emily felt a wave of gladness when Thunder nodded. "Will you be fine on your own? I want to check out my Diamond and I'd hate to disturb you if you'd like to hang out with other ponies."

"Sure! Go ahead."

As Emily rushed to the Crowns' building, she heard a soft voice from inside the stables. It was of a horse, saying, "How about we do something fun together?"

Then she heard Thunder's familiar voice agreeing. "Okay, maybe a canter somewhere?"

Emily was happy that Thunder was joining in with everyone else and having a good time. She steered her eyes away from the stables and went in the direction of the Crowns.

The Crown Building was fairly short, a glossy, neat shade of white, and slightly square-shaped. Emily decided that she somewhat preferred the Crown Building to her small, cosy villa by the countryside meadows. When Emily got inside, she looked around. The common area felt like a palace, with velvet carpets and armchairs. Large paintings of picturesque sceneries hung from the soothing grey walls, and the building was amply spacious.

She spotted a flight of spiralling marble stairs at the far end of the lobby and raced up it, following signs to the Rainbow Crown. When she got to its floor, she was greeted by Scarlet and Ella. They waved to her and then hurried away. One into a door with the name "Ella" on it and the other with the name "Scarlet" on

it, both patterned with gemstones, as it was Gemstone Crown. Emily saw a door patterned with rainbows with nameplates of Victoria, then Lily, then Ivy, and then . . . Emily! Emily read on, next to her Diamond's door. Her other neighbour was Abby, and then Isla! Emily was filled with happiness and excitement. Ivy was her closest friend, currently.

Emily pushed her door open and gasped. Her Diamond was awesome! It had pastel rainbow-coloured walls and a big bed. On the walls were watercolour paintings of meadows, the Academy's lesson buildings, sunsets, and rainbows. The paintings had platinum, opal, and gold frames. In the corner, there was a desk with a few books placed on it. Next to the bed was a bookshelf and a bedside table with some roses, dahlias, and chrysanthemums in a marble vase dotted with strawberry-coloured stones. Emily giggled playfully as she ran a hand over the chrysanthemums' uneven layers of petals.

Right, she thought after smelling the ruby-red roses, *it's time to see what else my Diamond has to offer!*

Emily got up and hopped onto her bed. She bounced off the springy mattress and skipped to a large bookshelf on her wall. It held dozens of colorful books, all filed neatly in alphabetical order. Next to it was a mini dining table with gold napkin holders and silverware. Emily looked across to find a pink sofa. Emily sat on it and found it to be soft and bouncy. Her Diamond was the best! She put her turquoise laptop on her bedside table and started to charge it. Then, she turned on the air conditioner and sat down on her bed, looking out the enormous glass window and into the Mini Playground when she remembered what she was here for!

She leapt off her bed, almost crushing her fluffy magenta home slippers that were by the bed and ran to a little bulletin board. Sure enough, a timetable was hanging on it. Emily's eyes scanned the timetable.

She read:

Tuesday: Cooking (9:45 – 10:50), Mathematics (11:15 – 12:00), Environmental Studies (12:20 – 1:20), Horse Racing (1:30 – 2:00).

Emily was thrilled. Cooking was her favourite subject! She sighed when she read *horse racing,* reassuring herself that it was only for half an hour. After reading the whole timetable, Emily decided it was time to hang out with her new friends and their pets.

As Emily walked out of the Crown building, she saw some girls with their cats. She recognized River, her wavy, golden hair bouncing off her shoulders. River was chatting with another girl. She had brown hair and a shimmery, hot pink hairband. The girls spotted Emily and smiled welcomingly. "Hello!" the girl with brown hair exclaimed. "My name is Lisa. Wait . . . aren't you the girl I met at lunch?"

"Oh yes! Hi again, Lisa," Emily said.

"I was just about to go to the pet collection section with my friend River. Would you like to join us? It would be lovely to have a new friend along with us, won't it, River?"

River nodded. "Yes! I can't wait for you to see our cats. They're just too cute!"

Emily beamed at the girls. They were very friendly. "Sure! I can't wait to see them. My horse, Thunder, says that cats are the most popular pets in the world. Is that true?"

Lisa nodded.

"I just checked the timetable. The last class for today is horse racing, but I'm confused. If you two have cats, it'll be pretty . . . difficult to ride them," Emily said, stifling a grin.

"Oh, of course," said River. "You and all the other horse owners have that timetable. Cat owners have a different timetable. The same goes for dog, pegasi, and unicorn owners."

Emily understood. "Well, thanks. Should we go see—"

"Our cats!" River and Lisa chorused with a high-five.

Emily, Lisa, and River hopped along and in about ten minutes, the three girls reached the pet collection building. There were a few cats playing on jungle-gyms and scratching posts. A black and white cat who was leaping across his sleeping mother caught River's eye. She waved.

"Leo, darling!" she said. "Come to me, sweetie. Did you enjoy lunch? I thought you two might like it in here instead." The kitten bounded towards River and rubbed against her eight times. He leapt in her arms and was about to lick her when his mother climbed on River, too, and pawed him. Leo meowed happily and swatted Xena purposely with his tail.

"You naughty little one!" River cooed and her eyes sparkled as Leo jumped and sat on top of Xena.

Leo meowed and said, "River, let's go to the Mini Playground!" He jumped out of River's arms and was closely followed by Xena.

Emily waved at the two cats, trying to make a good first impression.

Xena looked at Emily and smiled. "Hello. I am Xena, and you are?"

Emily smiled back. "Hello, Xena." Xena was so sweet! "I am Emily from Rainbow Crown." Emily sighed softly in contentment. Everything was perfect.

Little did she know what lay ahead of her . . .

Chapter 11

The Beginning of Adventure

After a few hours spent in meeting animals and playing, Emily grew a little tired. "This has been so much fun," she said, stifling a yawn. "But I think I better go to the stables and . . ." She gasped and said, "Oh dear! I'm so late! Thunder must be upset with me. Let's have some fun again soon."

Though River, Lisa, Xena, and Leo looked like they would have at least wanted to play for another hour, Lisa smiled gently and said, "Of course, Emily. It's been so much fun hanging out with you, but I think you really need to go. And don't worry. I'm positive that your horse won't be upset with you at all!"

Emily began to run. "Thank you, but I doubt it. Bye, everyone!" With one last wave, she sped off to the stables.

When she arrived, she noticed that Thunder was facing his stall's window.

"Thunds! Hi! What's . . ." Emily trailed off as Thunder whipped around, looking exasperated. He stomped a hoof and then neighed, whinnied twice, whickered once, and turned his back on Emily.

". . . up?" Emily said, a little nervous.

"What took you so long?" Thunder snorted. "I have been waiting here for hours. All the horses, unicorns, and pegasi went for a huge gallop to Bloom Hills and I'm still here! Can't we go for a gallop now that you are," Thunder paused dramatically, "finally, here?"

Emily's face fell. What? I lost track of time and Thunder missed an entire gallop because of me? she thought, feeling awful.

"Oh, sorry," she said, petting Thunder's muzzle apologetically. "I got so caught up, and I lost track of time . . ." Her voice trailed off as Thunder snorted and looked away. He knelt down and picked up some hay.

"Look, I'd never do this on purpose. You're my best friend!" Emily protested, her hand reaching to pet Thunder.

Thunder stopped chewing and looked up. His face softened, and he nickered fondly. "Obviously you didn't do that on purpose! Even I get carried away sometimes. I forgive you; you didn't mean to be this late."

"Really, Thunds?" she asked softly. Thunder winked playfully and said, "Of course! Who am I to huff about my rider making new cat friends?"

Emily brushed the hay off her face and spat some out of her mouth. "Thunder, thank you so much. Honestly, I was afraid of messing up our friendship. But what can make up for a gallop to Bloom Hills, I wonder . . ."

Thunder whickered. "I have to admit, a gallop sounded good, but we can do something else fun to celebrate our first day at Animal Academy." Emily grinned. "I'll open your stall and we can do something fun. How about we . . ." She stopped. "Er, I honestly don't know."

"It's a little late. Should we do something small like a visit to the library and Pet Spa?" Thunder suggested. His ears pricked. "I really want to pick up a book or two about horses' tack. Also, I have been searching for a reason to gallop in that tunnel again!"

"Okay! That sounds good. Let's go!" Emily was happy that Thunder was not too upset with her about missing the gallop. She mounted onto her horse, and even though she didn't feel like riding that much, she was happy to be with Thunder.

At that moment, she came up with a good reason to ask Thunder to not ride fast. "Thunder, maybe we should not gallop, since it's nearly dinner." Emily stroked Thunder's brown mane and fiddled with the jades beaded in it. "That way we won't get tired," she continued, "and so we can spend some time together at dusk and then say goodnight."

Thunder swished his tail and nodded.

"Okay," he said. "That is a smart plan to save energy. And I do want to spend time with you at dusk."

"Amazing," said Emily cheerfully. "Let's go!"

After a few minutes, the two were in the secret tunnel. After pacing through the tunnel for a bit, Emily grew tired and was relieved when Thunder said, "Here's the end of the tunnel!"

As Emily caught her breath, she noticed a hole above her. Light filtered in from the way outside. There was a flash of purple. Emily stood very still for a second. She then rubbed her eyes and looked at the light again. "I think something's out there!" she whispered to Thunder.

"Okay. Let me take a look," Thunder said and peered out. "No one there, Emily. You must be imagining things."

"Are you cer—"

"Yes."

Thunder cantered out the passageway and called to Emily. As she stepped out of the tunnel, Emily cautiously looked around, but, as Thunder had said, no one was there.

I must have been imagining things, she assured herself.

Emily and Thunder now ran in the direction of the library. Emily entered inside and gasped. Hundreds of shelves were packed with thick and thin books of all genres and placed neatly in alphabetical order. The library was filled with velvet arm chairs, desks, and long sofas.

Knocking on the window to get Thunder's attention, she exclaimed, "The library is amazing!"

Thunder was grazing on some fresh grass. He peeked inside the library and nodded absently. "Like the library, this ryegrass I've found is also amazing," he said, munching on a tuft of grass.

Emily was browsing through some books when she heard someone giggle, making her jump in surprise.

"Shh, this is a library," someone said, her head buried inside a big, blue book. "No shouting, please!"

Emily's head whipped around. She had completely forgotten that other people might be in the library, too! She cringed, embarrassed that someone had heard her yelling to her horse inside the library, telling him that it's amazing!

The girl put the book down.

"Oh! It's you, Ivy!" Emily exclaimed.

"Oh! It's you, Em!" Ivy said at the same time.

"What are you doing here?" she asked. "Ivy, you like to read?"

Ivy laughed. "Who doesn't? I love reading essays, and this book about something called a Flash-Hoof Pony is especially interesting!"

Emily sat down on the magenta beanbag and read with Ivy. The book said:

The Flash-Hoof Pony is a rare creature with magical superspeed powers and the ability to start fires anywhere with its flaming horns. They are usually mares who live in rainforests and are not gentle in nature. Their hooves are purple, eyes are green, and their magical powers are unparalleled. The speed of the Flash-Hoof Pony is said to be the greatest of all creatures in existence. Only one animal has been known to catch up with the Flash-Hoof Pony—a horse who had been trained to outrun it!

Humans who have had the chance to see the Flash-Hoof Pony, reported that it ran so fast, it was only visible as a flash of purple.

Emily's heart skipped a beat. She had seen a flash of purple just a few minutes ago. Could that have been a Flash-Hoof? She continued to read the book and talk with Ivy, but her mind kept wondering if she had actually witnessed a rare, mythical creature.

When they had finished reading the book, Emily began to confess, "Ivy, you know, just like in this book, I saw a—" She paused, wondering if she should tell Ivy about the flash of purple she had seen earlier. No, Emily decided. I'll keep it a secret. Thunder wouldn't want me to tell anyone! "Oh, I just saw a . . . a cloud. Shaped like . . . a heart. I thought I should tell you that!" She was telling the truth: she had seen a heart-shaped cloud and wanted to tell Ivy about it.

Emily smiled at Ivy. "This has been so much fun," she said.

"But I should go. Thunder's outside, waiting for me. Oh! That reminds me: he wants me to pick up a few books for him. I think I should also get him reading horseshoes. Do you know what they are?"

"No."

"They're horseshoes with special sticky bottoms that help horses flip pages."

"Awesome! That's a really cool invention!" exclaimed Ivy.

"I agree," said Emily, before hurrying to the horse section of books. She picked up one book about tack, as Thunder had asked, and two books from the series The Galloping Cartwheels. She read the synopsis, which said that the book was about three girls, Lyla, Lillian, and Addison, who were fond of doing horseback gymnastics.

"This looks like something Thunder would enjoy reading!" Emily gushed, holding up one of the books for Ivy to see.

"Wow," said Ivy. "Do you have time to read the

first chapter with me?"

"I think I'll have to go now, Ivy. Thunder and I want to go to the Pet Spa. It sounds fun!"

She picked up two pairs of reading horseshoes with the help of Ms. Chantal, the librarian, and ran to the exit.

Ivy looked a little disappointed, but then she perked up. "Okay, but let's go to dinner later, agreed? And let's sit next to each other!"

"Agreed!"

Emily nodded and gave Ivy a quick hug. "Bye, Ivy!" she said as she passed by the great library doors. Emily walked outside and saw Thunder talking with Lavender. He turned to Emily and said, "Did you meet Ivy? Lavender told me she was in the library."

"Yes, I sure did!" Emily said. She got onto Thunder.

"And are you super thrilled to go to the spa, now?" he asked.

"Oh yes! It's going to be so much fun!" she whooped. "I can't wait to get to the Pet Spa!"

"I really want my mane re-braided," Thunder said. He started to gallop to the Pet Spa, and for once, Emily didn't mind Thunder going fast. After thirty seconds, they had arrived. He sighed, content. "Wow, we're here! The spa looks even more amazing than I imagined!" Emily was flabbergasted.

"I think I see a few other ponies in there, too. And three or four kittens! We may become friends with them. Bonus!" Thunder laughed, nudged the door open and gasped.

"Oh, my goodness!" he said as he sauntered into the clean, glimmering spa. Emily slid off his back and strode to a shelf in the corner. "This seems like the spa menu," she said, pointing to it.

Thunder neighed in utter delight as he grabbed the menu with his mouth. "Hmm . . . Okay. I'm getting the deep-sea massage, honey-hoof glitter run, mer-pony splash, which seems like it's a dive into cleansing and calming bubbles.

Ooh, I'm also going to do the silk twinkle mane wash and also the—"

"Thunds! No more!" Emily said, laughing. "You'll look like a shiny brown peach at the end of all this! Now, let's find those four rooms and get done by six-forty."

Using a map at the back of the menu, Emily guided Thunder to a stall that said: Deep Sea Massage.

Thunder happily went in. "Wow!" He gazed at the shimmering white walls and crystalline chandeliers. "I feel like I'm royalty!" His eyes darted to the ceiling, which was covered with coral-patterned wallpaper.

"I think that soft carpet is where you should wait, Thunder. I'll check the personnel room for the bubble massage and see if anyone's there," Emily said. She looked at Thunder, who was still marvelling at the chandeliers.
"Thunder!"

Thunder jumped out of his thoughts and

nodded. He sat on a straw mat and closed his eyes, ready to be groomed.

Emily was about to go into the personnel room when she noticed a lady, with short orange hair and a blue dress, standing there. "Hello," she greeted. "I am Ms. Charlotte. I run the pet spa. What's your name?"

"My name is Thunder."

"And mine is Emily."

Emily watched Ms. Charlotte carefully as she took out some foaming wash and rubbed it on Thunder. She kept rubbing for five minutes and then mixed some pastel-coloured petals in the bubbles. After some time, Ms. Charlotte washed everything off with rosewater.

Drenched, Thunder shook himself, wetting Emily. She sighed and wiped herself using a towel that kind Ms. Charlotte gave her.

After Thunder had been cleaned and dried off, he sparkled and twinkled brighter than Emily's golden ballet shoes! Emily's eyes widened when she looked at him. She wrapped her arms around him and said, "You look like a gold coin!"

"Thank you," said Thunder, pleased.

Thunder thanked Ms. Charlotte, too, and then turned to Emily. "What next?"

"Now, let's do a mane wash for you! I can see some dust in it, and it's tangled. Most of your plaits have opened, too. Come on!"

She rode Thunder to the silk twinkle mane wash room. A teacher was sitting on a chair, reading a thick black and golden book titled *The Art of Colour*. "Oh, hello!" she said, putting her book away. "I believe you're Emily and Thunder?"

"Yep, but how did you know?" asked Thunder. "I'm also the art teacher, so we know everyone, because at the end of term one we paint special portraits of you to hang up in your Diamonds," the teacher replied. "Well, Thunder and Emily, I'm Ms. Rissa."

Once Thunder had had his plaits opened, Ms. Rissa sprayed cucumber and Lemon Blossom water on his mane and brushed it with a sparkly silver brush. She put some white shampoo-gel on the ends of Thunder's mane and rubbed it in. She then rinsed it with water and got the dust out of it. Next came the bubbly purple, maple-syrup-scented water that Ms. Rissa massaged onto Thunder's entire mane. It was rubbed in thoroughly on every strand of Thunder's hair and Ms. Rissa kept on brushing it with the silver brush. She beaded orange and blue beads in Thunder's mane instead of the usual jades and emeralds.

He tapped his hooves on the ground impatiently when Ms. Rissa started combing his mane for the fourth time.

Soon, Ms. Rissa walked out of the room and returned with fancy rubber bands for Thunder. One had a dolphin, the other five had clouds, seven rubber bands had flowers and the rest had rainbows and star patterns.

From these, Thunder picked his favourites: two clouds, five stars, one rose, a Blaze Bloom flower, and the last one a dolphin.

Ms. Rissa beamed after plaiting Thunder's mane. "Good choice, and, Thunder, your mane looks fabulous! Now, Thunder and Emily, it's six-thirty and the spa will close soon, so how about you all trot along to dinner in Rainbow Crown's Dinner Lounge and eat?"

Thunder frowned. It was clear to Emily that he wanted to stay for a little longer. *Oh no. He is going to start arguing in front of a teacher!* Before he could voice his thoughts, Emily asked Ms. Rissa, "Ms. Rissa, do you have any idea where the lounge is?"

The words came out a little louder than she had intended. Ms. Rissa looked at Emily for a few seconds, amused. Then she answered, "The floor above your Diamonds. It's incredibly beautiful, you know, and easy to locate."

Emily thanked Ms. Rissa and rode out of the Pet Spa. "It's been a lovely day, hasn't it, Thunder?" she asked.

"Yes, it really has been," Thunder replied, staring at the darkening sky and the orange ball of sun setting in the horizon. Emily looked at her beautiful, strong horse in awe. Wasn't Thunder perfect? He sure was!

Chapter 12

The End of the Day

"Let's go! Lead the way to the Crown building," Emily said, putting her hand on Thunder. She rode him towards the Crown building after they had climbed out of the tunnel. "Okay, Thunder. Go on to the stables. Ms. Rissa told me that dinner for horses is served there. There will be apples, oats, and jaggery squares in your feed box. Finish it all and try to have some water from the lake behind the stables. Bye, Thunder. I'll come and see you right before I go to bed." Thunder whinnied and Emily dropped a quick kiss on his rosewater-scented forehead before running off to join her friends in the dinner lounge.

Emily pushed the door to the entrance of the Crown's building. This time, she didn't go into her Diamond. She ran all the way to the end of the velvet carpet and stopped. She looked around, searching for a staircase. At last! Emily's eyes strayed to the left side of the building, where only Shimmer Crown's Diamonds were. She caught sight of a tall, white marble staircase and immediately started to climb it.

Once Emily reached the top of the staircase, she spotted a huge rainbow-coloured door. The plate on it said: RAINBOW CROWN: DINNER LOUNGE.

As soon as Emily found the door, she darted inside. She felt warm and fuzzy once she stepped into the lovely, warm lounge.

"Emily! You still have your riding boots on! Get into something cleaner and then get inside," a voice said.

Emily followed the voice and turned around. She saw Isla, Abby, Lily, and Victoria standing in their pajamas and wearing fluffy slippers. Victoria's slippers were blue, Isla's were green, Abby's were orange, and Lily's were yellow. Emily noticed Ivy was not in the lounge yet. "Go on, Emily, or we might have to mop the floor!" Isla said dramatically. "You've not changed out of these boots since you rode to the spa."

Emily nodded and walked out of the lounge. *I have to find a washroom.* There wasn't one around. She was left with no choice but to go back to her Diamond. It took Emily a minute to find the restroom in her Diamond, and once she entered it, she couldn't help but take a deep breath. The air inside smelt like fresh cherry blossoms, buttercream, roses, and chocolate-caramel ice cream. Emily inhaled it in for a few seconds and then stepped into the marble bathtub. She turned on the hand-shower and sprayed fresh, room temperature water on herself. She took some mint-scented soap and rubbed it on herself. After rinsing everything off, she grabbed a lime-coloured towel patterned with turquoise, gold, and pink flamingos and dried herself off. Emily pulled her night-top over her head. It was light blue with bright yellow, emerald green, and silver stripes. She put on violet-blue pajamas with white stars printed on it. She remembered how her suitcase had had no space left for clothes, but she had squeezed everything in it in order to fit that top, as that was her night suit set for celebrations. And coming to Animal Academy was an absolute celebration.

Emily plopped on her soft, bouncy bed that had a magenta blanket spread on it. A smile lit up her face. Magenta was her favourite colour! She looked at her bedside table, and sitting there, was a big heart-shaped framed photo of her and Thunder! Emily squealed in delight, and bounced off her bed, tripping over her fluffy magenta slippers. She hurriedly put them on and rushed out her door, back to the lounge. This time Ivy was there, too, along with the rest of Rainbow Crown.

"Dinnertime!" Victoria sang. "What have we got?"

Abby hurried in, carrying four heavy baskets. "Sushi and soup!" she replied, panting a little. The fourth basket was huge, loaded with bottles of sauce and bowls of soup. "Um, a little help here?" Abby huffed. "There are about twenty types of sushi in here—"

"Nuh-uh," Isla spoke. "There are literally a billion sushi in here!"

The entire Rainbow Crown burst out laughing. "Isla!" Abby giggled. Suddenly she paused and then raised her voice, trying to imitate Isla. "I might as well drop the bags, which, I tell you, are so heavy, that if I do drop them . . ." Abby paused theatrically and flung her arms in the air, "the floor will crack, the doors will shake, the—"

That sent the girls of Rainbow Crown into peals of laughter again. "Isla, really!" Lily said. "You know there are only twenty types of sushi in there. To name one, there are California rolls, my favourite. Anyway, speaking of which, I'm starving! Anyone else hungry?"

Immediately, everyone chorused, "I AM!"

Lily grinned and turned to Isla. Her eyes twinkled as she said, "Come on! Go help Abby with unloading the sushi while I place the tablemats with Victoria."

Lily loves giving instructions, Emily noticed with a smile.

"I'll get the cutlery!" Ivy volunteered.

Emily raised her hand. "I'll go too!" Her best friend gave her a quick smile and then hurried off to the cupboard where the cutlery was. She opened the cupboard and all the cutlery fell out, covering Ivy's legs completely.

"Lucky that the knives weren't in this cupboard," Isla said. "Come on, hurry, and set them up on the tables! You need to—"

"I got it." Ivy cleared all the cutlery away, picked it up, and put it in a marble sink. She got some washing soap and turned the tap on, saying, "We do need the cutlery to be clean."

Victoria smiled. "Thanks. Lily, how about we start with spreading the tablemats? I like the pink ones with m—"

A deafening shriek resounded in the room. It had come from another lounge nearby.

Isla, Victoria, and Emily exchanged panicked looks. They bolted to the door. Looking around, they spotted the Feather Crown lounge. They ran to see what had happened when their eyes fell on a shattered window. The girls of that Crown were looking horrified as they ran for cover.

Oh no!

"Everyone!" exclaimed Lily urgently as a flash of purple lit up the sky and the balcony door exploded, sending wood pieces rocketing everywhere. "Get to the bathroom as soon as possible!"

Filled with dread and worry, the girls darted to the bathroom.

BANG! BANG! BOOM! More furniture blew

up around everyone.

The lounge table burst into smithereens and soup hurled everywhere. Sliding, hair wet with tomato soup and legs wobbling, Emily tried to run for cover. She was almost at the bathroom door when a purple ribbon of light struck the tiny console next to the bathroom door. The television that stood there tumbled to the ground and broke into a hundred pieces, and the console's four legs shot into the air and soared right past Emily.

"Help!" yelled a girl with long blonde hair. A piece of wood had landed in front of her. She sprinted to the right, but there was another flash, and a jagged rock blocked her way. More pebbles from outside boomed in with another blaze of violet. "HELP!"

Emily flooded with determination. She remembered Thunder's epic leap over the spider-infested tree in the morning and knew that if her horse was so courageous, she could be too. She closed her eyes for a few seconds and focused. What should I do? She tried to think.

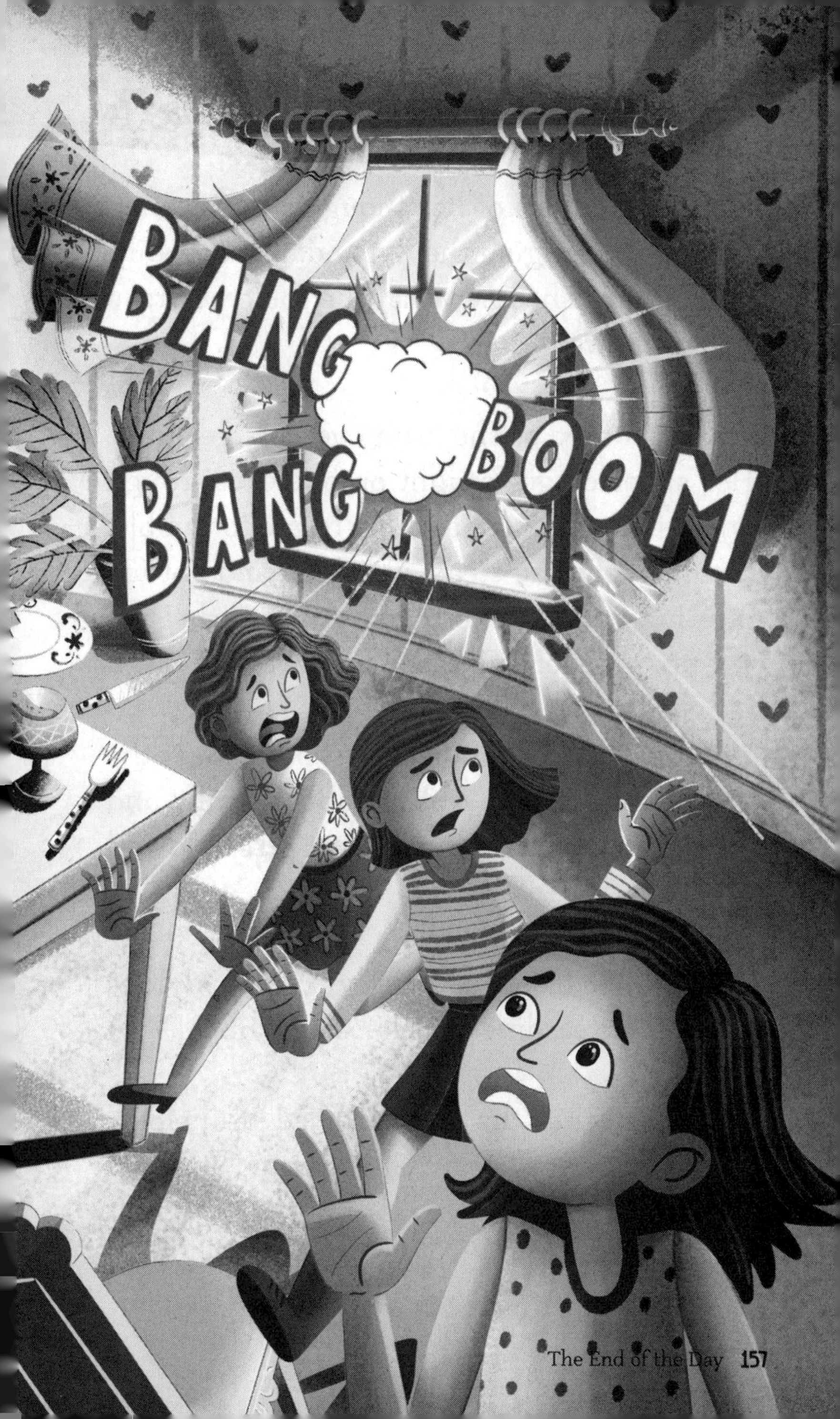
BANG
BANG
BOOM

"Somebody help, please!" the girl pleaded.

Emily jerked out of her thoughts and dashed to the girl, dodging the flying debris speedily. In her mind, she knew that she could be brave when she wanted to.

Emily grunted as she leapt over a large stone. Her shoelace got caught on one of its rough edges that stuck out and she began to tumble. Instinctively, she steadied herself and got up, offering her hand to the stranded girl. They got up together and raced for cover.

"In here!" Abby and Victoria shouted over the booms and cracks. Abby grabbed Emily and yanked her inside. The blond girl followed nervously.

"Is everyone okay?" asked Ivy. Everybody was packed like sardines in the bathroom.

"I am," breathed the girl Emily had just helped. "And my name's Daisy." She grinned at Emily gratefully.

"Nice name, and good that you're safe," said Isla. "That was terrifying! Now, let's go to a non-shattered lounge. Our's isn't that bad."

"Yep, we should probably shift as soon as possible," added Abby. "Looks like it won't be long before the bathroom's destroyed too."

"I agree with Abby," Ivy said. "Let's go now."

"Oh, it could have been so much worse," Clara said once everyone had moved into the Rainbow Crown Lounge. "Everyone is safe."

She smiled and looked around at everyone. "We just need to rebuild the windows and sofas and chairs and televisions and chandeliers and . . . huh. It's actually a lot."

Lily smiled comfortingly. "It's okay. No person could have broken the window, though. Something must have done it. Something that is fast. I couldn't make out what it was. Clara, Rose, Bella, Daisy, Ella, Grace, did you see anything unusual?"

Chapter 13
The Mystery Grows

Daisy looked mystified. "I'll tell you. It was mysterious and—"

Grace interrupted, "All we saw was a flash and the window cracked. And then we all panicked and screamed."

"No, there's more. There were more blazes and flashes when everything burst. Ooh! Could it be a student playing tricks?" Rose wondered, her eyes gleaming.

Lily looked lost in thought as she nodded vaguely. Emily could tell she wanted more detail. A few seconds later Lily asked, "What colour was the flash? Was it just plain white?"

Ella raised her hand and said, "The flash was definitely violet. Oh, and we saw some strands of dark purple hair. Does that tell us something? Maybe it was Frost, Daisy's unicorn. She has purple hair."

Daisy glared at Ella. "No way it's her!"

"But I'm certain it was a unicorn!" Ella snapped.

Emily felt butterflies in her tummy. She felt like she was stuck high on a Ferris wheel which had broken and would not move down anymore. She shot a worried look at Ivy and saw that she looked anxious, too. Emily walked over to Ivy and whispered, "You're my best friend, obviously you know that. I think I can tell you this one thing that I meant to tell you earlier, and which may help us solve this mystery . . ."

Emily explained everything in brief: the tunnel and her quick route to the cafeteria, and the flash she had seen when crawling out of it. She told Ivy about how Thunder thought she was seeing things. She didn't speak about her dislike of riding.

Ivy's eyes grew wider and wider at hearing all this. "Oh my! So do you mean—"

A bell chimed deafeningly, making Emily's heart leap.

"Oh my!" Victoria squeaked. "It's gotten late! Time for dinner, everyone. Actually, this bell means it's time to wrap up. Feather Crown, if you don't mind, can you eat in the cafeteria? Otherwise, it will get stuffy in here."

Feather Crown nodded and filed out the door, waving goodbye to their new friends.

Ivy nodded at Emily and then turned around. "I have something important I'd like to tell you all. Emily and I read a book about a dangerous pony, called the Flash-Hoof Pony, with a horn that is made of flames. They have superspeed and fire powers." Ivy explained everything, not leaving anything out.

Everyone's mouths dropped open.

"But how do we know for sure?" Victoria asked.

"Grace also said that she had seen dark purple strands."

Isla's eyes grew wide. "Don't you see? The Flash-Hoof Pony's mane is dark purple! It's got to be her!"

Abby smiled. "We are so close to solving this puzzle! But before we do, I think dinner sounds good."

Everyone nodded and sat down to dinner. Eating delicious avocado and cucumber sushi with soy sauce, the whole Rainbow Crown was talking all at once.

"It can't be though. Why would a Flash-Hoof Pony want to do that?" asked Abby.

Emily bit her lip. Abby was right. Why would the Pony want to do such a thing? Emily could hardly eat anything after that. She just wanted to get to the bottom of this!

"Dinner's over!" Victoria sang as she piled the silverware and plates in the basin and rubbed them with foamy soap that smelt like coconut butter.

Emily helped clean up, but her mind was still running wild with questions. She settled them with a sip of hot chocolate and a slice of fudgy chocolate brownie by the fireplace.

As Victoria turned on the radio, Isla clapped her hands to get everyone's attention. "I bet something mysterious is going to happen!" she

announced. "But don't worry. We'll stick together and solve the mystery no matter what. Right?"

Victoria nodded enthusiastically. "We'll definitely look out for each other. Isla's right. We have almost gotten to the bottom of this mystery, so we can't give up now!"

"And something scary may happen, you're right," said Ivy.

Lily picked up her mug of hot chocolate and nodded as she sat with the rest of the girls. "So, from now on, until we are sure that the Academy is safe, we have to stick together."

"Agreed!" chorused the rest of Rainbow Crown.

"And whatever comes in Rainbow Crown's way, we'll solve it and put it right!" Isla cried.

The girls cheered. Lily, in a moment of excitement, spilled hot chocolate on Abby's top. "Whoops!"

Emily's eyes began to droop, and she yawned. Abby fumbled for a cloth to wipe her top with. Wondering what the time was, she glanced at a clock. It was past nine. "Hey, everyone? It's almost half past nine," she said.

"Oh, that's late!" Isla exclaimed.

Abby giggled and stopped wiping her top for a moment. "So, I guess we should go to our Diamonds, right?"

"Yep! Goodnight, everyone," Emily said. She strode to the door. "Now, I promised Thunder I would go to the stables and say goodnight. I think I better leave now. We all have to be in our Diamonds by nine-thirty."

Rainbow Crown waved off Emily as she hurried down to the stables. Thunder was there, talking with a unicorn, who was right next to him. He beamed as he turned to Emily, and said, "Hello! Yum, dinner was good."

"Good to know. Goodnight, Thunder," Emily said softly, hugging him.

"Hey, look! The moon's looking so lovely," Thunder nickered all of a sudden. They both gazed in awe at the crescent moon gleaming in the dark sky and then looked at each other. "Sleep well. I'll see you in the morning." Emily dropped a kiss on Thunder's nose and patted him. "Bye, Thunder. Love you." Thunder neighed and smiled as Emily walked off, back to her Diamond.

As soon as Emily lay down on her bed, she drifted off to sleep. She didn't even realize that it was morning until Thunder came into the Diamond building and woke Emily up, even though horses weren't allowed in! It was now sharp nine o'clock.

Emily groaned as she sat up and started to comb her slightly wavy, brown hair. She wanted to sleep a little extra, but she wanted to be on time for her cooking lesson.

"Thunder, let's use the tunnel now, what do you say? Let's go!"

Once Emily reached the tunnel, she tapped on it, making sure that another person or animal was not in there. There was no answer, so Emily tried to open it. She tried to turn the knob. She also took a few steps back to not get hit by the door when it swung open. But instead, the door just stayed in place.

"It didn't open?" Thunder asked. "Try again."

Again, Emily tried to turn the knob. Again, the knob didn't turn.

"I-can't-seem-to-open it!" Emily panted through gritted teeth. Soon she gave up and asked Thunder to try. "I can't seem to either!" he complained. He tried tapping it with his hooves, but only sent a pile of books flying. "It's no use,"

said Emily, concerned.

"But why?" fretted Thunder. "I never knew it could lock! There may be someone in there!"

"Thunder . . . Thunder . . ." Emily whispered, pressing her ear against the wall. "I think someone is inside!"

"WHAT?" Thunder gasped. "How?"

"Did I not tell you what happened in the Feather Crown lounge?" Emily asked.

"No!"

"Sorry!" Emily told him about the explosions, the broken windows and furniture, and the chaos that followed afterwards. "And Ella said that the flashes were purple, the same colour as a Flash-Hoof Pony—"

"Oh my!" Thunder interrupted.

"There's got to be the Flash-Hoof Pony in there!" she emphasized. "Because they live in rainforests. A few may live in this one that's to one side of the Academy, don't you think? I'm not sure why, but I know they're also in the tunnel."

"Let's break into the tunnel and confront those non-unicorn unicorns!" Thunder scowled. "I'm ready."

After some time of pondering, Emily had reached a conclusion. "But I read that the ponies—"

"Non-unicorn unicorns," corrected Thunder.

"Okay," giggled Emily. "Well, I read that they are dangerous. When we confront them, we should do it as a team with friends. I think we—even you, Thunds—will be stronger as a team. No offense."

"None taken. What should we do instead?" Thunder asked. His eyes twinkled.

"I'm thinking."

"Me, too."

"Well, according to my watch, we should think faster."

"Just follow me." Thunder trotted off with Emily on his back. She enjoyed the wind in her hair as Thunder ran.

Soon, Emily was soaring high in the sky on Rocket, Isla's pegasus. Thunder was flying beside him, with a pair of brown wings that Saturn had made for him. Within five minutes, Emily had reached the cooking class with Ms. Ariella.

The next few days were enjoyable for Emily and Thunder. There were so many new things to learn, games to play, and places to go.

The window had been repaired in Feather Crown's lounge, but a horse called Meadow had found deep holes in the race paths. Ms. Smith had turned pale when she had gone to take a close look. "Oh no," she said. "These have definitely been made by someone who wants to hurt the horses. Everyone knows that if you step in one of these while running, you could hurt your hooves."

Emily couldn't help but think of the locked tunnel and the flashes of purple she had seen.

She told herself not to be silly, and that it may just have been a unicorn practising magic, not a Flash-Hoof Pony. But what if my wild thoughts are right? Emily asked herself from time to time. No. They can't be! A few more days passed, with Emily spending most of her time with Thunder. She was also having fun during lessons, and found the 'Environment is Ours' lesson to be most enjoyable for her. It was taught by Ms. Rosalee, who herself loved the subject.

"Today, we are going to learn about the Animal Academy rainforest," said Ms. Rosalee. Emily quickly noted down Animal Academy Rainforest using her best handwriting. Ms. Rosalee continued, "Thank you, everyone. As you may know, at Animal Academy, us teachers aim to teach you how to care and love your pets," she said. "We—" Suddenly, a snarl resounded from the back of the classroom. Everyone looked surprised. "Who was that?" she asked.

"NOT ME!" chorused the girls of Rainbow Crown.

Ms. Rosalee laughed, "Oh, okay then. It mustn't

have been anything. As I was saying, Animal Academy is all about caring for your pets. But there are dangerous animals in our rainforest as well. Now, one such animal is the Terplantatious. It has the power to freeze you. However, you can find a way to melt the ice it can throw at you. Using honey butter, sugar, or daisy powder will help with that. There is also another dangerous animal called the Flash-Hoof Pony." Ms. Rosalee then spoke at length about the kinds of menacing and harmless creatures that inhabit the rainforest.

Emily copied down every word.

After an hour, Ms. Rosalee said, "Okay! Goodbye everyone. See you next week!" At once, everyone filed out of the room.

Victoria said, "My parents live close by to the Academy, so I'll go spend the weekend there with Saturn. We're allowed to go to our homes over the weekend if they are less than an hour away, you know."

Emily nodded, a little distracted. She then hurried

to her Diamond and picked up the book titled *The Terplantatious*. Clutching the book tightly, she sat in the lounge and started to read. Lily came over to join her. "Cool!" Lily exclaimed. "A book of the dangerous animal we learnt about in class today! Can I have a peek?"

Emily was startled and shut the book in a hurry. She didn't want anyone else to see. She wanted to read this book so she could help solve a mystery.

"Um, I think this belongs to the library. I-It closes soon. Er, I'll . . . see you!" She turned on her heel and quickly stepped to the door. She swerved around the corner and darted to her Diamond. In record time, Emily bathed and got dressed in her pajamas.

Once she had changed, Emily couldn't wait any longer. She hurried over to the stables.

"Thunder, where are you?" said Emily, taking

several deep breaths. Her horse looked up from his hay and smiled.

Emily didn't wait to greet him. She flashed a small grin at him and said, "Sorry to come at such an odd hour. I'm just a little worried."

Thunder's ears pricked and his eyes flashed with concern. "What's the matter, Emily?"

"Thunds, I pieced it all together. A Flash-Hoof could have done all this; the evidence is that we—Rainbow and Feather Crown—saw strands of purple hair! That's like the only thing that proves that it was the Flash-Hoof Pony, you know." A shiver ran through her as she rushed through her explanation. She reminded Thunder about the flashes and the broken windows, putting it all together. She still didn't tell him about her fear of riding though; she didn't want to hurt his feelings.

Thunder's eyes widened, "Oh no—it makes perfect sense! The only question is . . . why would she want to do all this?"

Emily sighed. Honestly, she didn't have any answers. "Hmm. Let's see . . . they live in the rainforest. They like their own kind. They are not always gentle . . ."

Thunder stomped his hoof. "This is like a puzzle. Except it's almost like you lost a few pieces under your bed."

"Mm." Emily knitted her brow.

Thunder frowned, deep in thought.

"Wait! Emily!" he said suddenly. "You said it. They like their own kind. Right. There."

Emily's heart skipped a beat. "What do you mean?"

"Maybe they like their own kind a little too much. Maybe they only like themselves. They could be doing this to harm us and somehow . . . overpopulate their kind!"

Emily gasped. "You're right! That's a great theory. Imagine you were a haughty creature. You'd like your kind so much and find the others bothersome. Wouldn't you want to ensure your kind was safe from extinction? These creatures are smart."

Thunder nodded.

"But what about the Terplantatious?" said Emily.

"Who? The Turf-and-Gracious? The Terp-Land-Acious? Wait, the Temptations?"

"A special kind of turtle. Terplantatious," Emily

chuckled. "I have a book about them in my room. After reading a few pages, I discovered that they dwell in rainforests, too!"

"Are they as haughty as those Flash-Hoof Ponies, too?" Thunder enquired, sounding rather angry.

"Don't know, but I read they are vulnerable to other more powerful creatures, even though they can freeze things," Emily responded.

"Whoa, freeze things?" said Thunder incredulously. "And they're vulnerable?"

"Well, the Flash-Hoof Ponies' horns are made of flames. Flames can melt ice!" Emily pointed out. Thunder suddenly gulped. "I bet they've teamed up together so that they are no threat to one another. The Ponies want more of their kind and must have forced a few Terplantatiousi to help!"

"Oh-my-wow. You could be right! This must be what's going on." Emily paused. "I'm going to tell my friends and ask them for help. They are in their Diamonds."

Thunder nodded. "Hmm. Let's hold an urgent

meeting tomorrow morning." He pointed his muzzle to the sun, now setting, its orange, red, and yellow hues making the sky glow. In the distance, an owl sat on Thunder's hay, hooting every few seconds. Emily strolled to it and stroked its feathers.

"Emily," Thunder said, excited now, "did you know that the teachers allow sleepovers with your pets on weekends? I just remembered and I want one now!"

"Yes! Me too!" Emily agreed, ecstatic.

Emily sat down on a straw bed next to Thunder. They chatted for almost an hour and then fell asleep.

"Wake up!"

Emily slowly opened her eyes. She hugged Thunder, who was playing with Emily's hair through his hooves.

"WAKE UP!"

Thunder now stood on Emily's ponytail. She squeaked as he pulled her hair. Maybe a sleepover wasn't a good idea after all. Emily suddenly burst out laughing as someone tickled her. Her eyes squinted and opened. "Oh! Ivy! What's up?"

"No time."

Emily scrambled to her feet at hearing the anxiety in Ivy's voice.

Before Emily could say anything else, Ivy dragged Emily outside, with Lavender and Thunder following behind. Victoria came running up to them. "I couldn't go to stay with my parents," she said in dismay. "The car froze right before I got into it!" Victoria's words were like a cold splash of water. All sleepiness evaporated from Emily's mind and worry surged through her brain instead. Thunder looked taken aback as well.

Ivy bit her lip and said slowly, "Lavender overheard your conversation with Thunder yesterday. You must be right."

"Th-thanks, I do think I'm correct," Emily stuttered.

"But just about ten minutes ago, Lavender and I were taking our morning ride when we found ... well ..." Ivy pointed shakily behind a bush.

Right there, just before Emily's eyes, sat a giant turtle whose shell gleamed orange. "The Terplantatious!" she cried. Thunder neighed and reared up. "I've heard the detention room is always under lock and key. It'd just take a wheelbarrow to carry you into that room and lock you up. Want to be imprisoned forever?"

The turtle's eyes widened. He glared at them, growling ferociously. "What do you think about being frozen forever?" With one raise of its flipper, a white light covered Thunder. "Emily!

Help me! Help—"

Thunder's half-finished sentence left Emily flooded with alarm and horror. "NO! THUNDER!" she screamed. Her own horse was frozen! What should she do? She blinked back some tears. How could she bear to be without her dear horse for even a second?

She was absolutely terrified but managed to calm herself down by taking a few deep breaths. She suddenly spotted some daisies nearby and picked and shredded them until they turned into powder. The ice slowly began to melt as Emily sprinkled the powder onto her horse.

"Please work," breathed Emily, her eyes looking dearly at Thunder as the ice began to melt slightly. Emily's heart thudded against her chest as she sprinkled the last of the powder onto Thunder. "Please work, please work, please work." She stepped forward and hugged her horse.

Emily sucked in her breath as the ice cover fell to the ground, shattering into a million tiny pieces. Swiftly, Thunder shook off all the ice-cold water. "I-I'm free!" gasped Thunder as he caught his breath. Emily hopped backwards in delight. Thunder staggered to Emily and buried his face in her hair. "You freed me, Emily!" he nickered, nuzzling his rider. "Thank you! You freed me with that daisy powder! How smart of you."

Emily gave Thunder a tight hug. "I will always

protect my wonderful horse."

The Terplantatious cackled. "You freed Blunder. Whatever. I can freeze and re-freeze until you've picked all the daisies in the world."

"Wait and see—we'll stop you from all this dark magic in a hoofbeat," Thunder snapped. "And, it's Thunder."

The turtle raised his flipper. "I don't care what your name is. You, girl in the stripey top, let me freeze you first."

Emily froze, realizing that the Terplantatious was pointing at her. "What? No!" She moved a few steps back, shielding her face with her hands.

Suddenly, a thundering sound shook the ground. It was Magic Crown!

"Oh no you don't!" Tisa barked and charged full speed at the turtle, even though June was yelling at her not to.

"You'll get frozen!" said June frantically. "Please stop, Tisa!"

Tisa ignored her. She snarled and stomped her paw on a pile of leaves. "I was in the doggy park when I saw you at the back of the 'Environment is Ours' building! I know you were there."

Chapter 14
Danger!

The turtle's eyes gleamed. It was an evil glint which gave Emily goosebumps.

"Well, can some dog see me? Sure. Can you fight with me? Well, you should have thought this through!" He raised his flipper and sent white light around Tisa. Tisa shrieked and June ran to Tisa, and scooped her up in her arms. June bolted away, muttering a scolding or two at Tisa, who looked untroubled at the fact that she had almost got frozen.

"Oh, you wicked monster!" Lisa screamed, glaring at the Terplantatious. "I got you, Terplantatious. Show him what you can do, Xena!"

Xena's eyes sparkled. She took out her claws and carefully poked the turtle. The turtle moaned. "Is that all you can do? I can freeze you, you know." Xena looked perplexed.

"Umm . . . and I can do . . . er . . . this?" She scratched the turtle's shell. The turtle rolled his eyes.

"Okay, weird scratcher thing—Zia, I think, back off and stay right there. I'll just go ahead and . . ."

Leo arrived at the scene and hissed ferociously. River was right behind him, trying to protect everyone from being frozen.

"Stop, River! Everyone is safe," Tisa exclaimed suddenly.

"Tisa, no, stop distracting River," June said, annoyed. "Please! Really, no one is safe."

"Ju, they are," Tisa said in a calm tone, her eyes shining.

June cast a puzzled look at Tisa. Emily tensed as the Terplantatious crept forward.

"We're safe here," Tisa repeated. "Safe at the school."

"Everyone, continue!" shouted someone. "The Terplantatious is here!"

"He'll freeze us all!"

"We're doomed!"

"Stay calm! Listen to me!" bellowed Tisa. She lowered her voice. "We're all going to be safe at the end. It's because the friendship between pets and their owners is the strongest friendship ever. Any bond which is strong and unbreakable is like a protective shield. We've got each other." Emily's heart slowed down.

"So, let's make sure we stay together," Tisa declared. "We'll be fine at the end of the day because our bonds are strong, even more so than an evil spell or dark magic! We'll show you what I mean, right?"

Everyone chorused a loud, "YES!"

Suddenly, out of nowhere, a flash of purple struck the ground and made everyone jump. "Oh no!" said Lily. "The Flash-Hoof Pony!" Rapidly, Emily told everyone about the flashes she had seen, but still not about her fear of riding. "And I believe it was the Flash-Hoof Pony that shattered the window!" she finished. Everyone gasped.

"Let's get into action!" Isla stomped her foot. "NOW!"

"STOP right there!" the Terplantatious yelled ferociously. "I will freeze you all, and now I mean it!" He lifted both his flippers. There was a crack and white light spiralled out of them. Acting fast, Saturn—Victoria's unicorn—let a huge gust of wind out from her horn. The white ice light was forced to change direction, flying towards the Terplantatious and freezing him over.

There was silence.

"Will you unfreeze him with daisy powder?"

Ivy asked Emily.

"Maybe soon," Emily replied.

Honey, Kate's kitten, piped up. "We could try becoming their friends?" he suggested. "It may work out."

"It may," June said, sounding a little skeptical. "But only may. Protecting the Academy and its students and teachers comes first, and we barely have any time." She stood on an upturned bucket and raised her voice. "Who's with me?"

"Me!" yelled all the students.

June looked firm. "Good. So, let's go—what are you waiting for?"

Just then, a loud neigh erupted, startling everyone. Emily clutched Ava's hand tightly. Everyone screamed. Emily felt Thunder tense.

We were right. Emily's heart beat loudly.

"RUN!" screamed Victoria, clutching her heart.

"Stay there!" the Flash-Hoof Pony yelled. "It's me, the magnificent Whirl-Fire! I'm the fastest Flash-Hoof Pony in the universe!"

She swished her tail snootily, holding a superior look which Emily instantly disliked.

"With my sister, Wild-Wind, and my other . . ." she looked around in disrespect, "inadequate sidekicks, we will threaten—"

She broke off as the Terplantatious growled, "You're the inadequate one."

Whirl-Fire snorted indignantly. She said nothing to the Terplantatious but continued speaking. "We will threaten all the animals out of this Academy, and they will have no choice but to . . ." she paused here with an evil look in her eyes and cackled. "Well, pains me to say it, but you'll just have to give up this pointless pet school!"

Emily sucked in her breath. *Animal Academy is not pointless!*

Suddenly Whirl-Fire swerved around and snapped, "Ugh! Inferno over there is so slow!"

She was glowering at a tough tiger with turquoise stripes and glowing paws. "Hurry up!" Whirl-Fire smiled a twisted smile and said, "This is Inferno. He's a sky tiger, and his magic powers let him create boulders that can destroy anything! Get on my back, Inferno!"

Whirl-Fire poked Inferno using her horn made

up of purple flames. Just as Inferno, the sky tiger, got onto Whirl-Fire's back, Lisa said, "Poor Inferno! It must be horrible for him to be forced to listen to Whirl-Fire."

The Flash-Hoof Pony spun around and charged towards the building, shouting, "Fire away, Inferno!" Inferno looked tense as he lifted his paw up. Boulders were beginning to form in the sky.

Emily and Thunder exchanged looks.
Emily's heart skipped a beat. She couldn't bear for the boulders to break Animal Academy. Never!

She needed to speed to the main building of the Academy and stop the rocks . . . somehow. But how would she get there in time?

Emily forced herself to speak, even though she really didn't want to. But they had to gallop, and she simply couldn't be afraid. She needed to tell Thunder that she didn't enjoy riding so their bond could be stronger "Thunder!" she said, hugging her horse. "I . . . I fear riding.

I was never good at jumping and riding a horse. . . it always made me nervous. I'm sorry. I know you wish you could just go back to your home without me, but I don't like riding—I just haven't learnt a lot about it properly yet, and I wouldn't bear having any other horse but you. I wish I could be a perfect rider." She buried her face in Thunder's mane, waiting for a reply.

Thunder looked at her for a second, puzzled. His mouth opened to say something, but he stopped and took a deep breath.

"That's fine," he said finally. "I understand how you feel."

"I—wait, what?" Emily was shocked for a second. "You don't mind?"

"I don't, promise." Thunder took another deep breath. "But we must save the Academy. Please!"

Emily bit her lip. Ride, ride, ride, her brain kept repeating.

"Okay," she sighed. Her heart beat faster. "We have

to save the school!" As she felt her confidence grow, Emily noticed someone running towards her.

"What are you doing?" called River, from Shimmer Crown. "You're the fastest group in the Academy. A boulder has already broken a top turret of Feather's office and the dome above the Crown Building. You two have no choice but to stop the boulders quickly before they destroy the rest of the Academy."

"But Emily—" Thunder began.

"—wants to save the Academy," Emily said with pure determination. Her eyes blazed like fire. Deep down inside, her heart tingled with an unexpected rush of courage. She still felt a little jittery about riding, but at that moment she trusted Thunder more than ever, and all she focused on was saving the Academy.

"Really, Emsy?" Thunder nickered.

"Yes!" Emily glowed. She felt like she had just been splashed with a delicious feeling of hope.

Thunder arched his neck happily. "You are right," he breathed. "This is our school and saving it is our duty. Let's go!"

Emily jumped onto Thunder. He ran faster than a rocket! His hooves pounded on the ground every split second and he was gaining onto Whirl-Fire.

Suddenly, Tisa sprinted behind them and soon caught up. She gave them a colourful, net-like cloth. "This is a solid cloth-net June's cousin stitched," she said, panting. "Stop the boulders!"

Whirl-Fire reared viciously. Inferno then fired a humungous boulder at the Academy's main building, which was about a mile away. "Not so fast!" cried Thunder.

"We're more powerful than you will ever be!" exclaimed Emily fiercely. She had never been this

brave before. As the words left Emily's mouth, Thunder whinnied and threw the solid rainbow-like cloth across. It caught on a creeper's thorn and stood like a volleyball net. The boulder fired towards the school. Emily gasped. The rainbow blocked the boulder's path, and it catapulted the other way, hurtling into the rainforest.

Crash! Emily covered her ears as she heard a sound that sounded like a rock breaking, and a few shrieks. The boulder was now out of sight. Her heart slowed down in relief.

"Inferno!" Whirl-Fire was definitely not relieved. "You inane beast! I'll—"

Inferno snarled and jumped off Whirl-Fire's back. He ran back into the rainforest. Looking over his shoulder, he said, "I wanted to be a part of this vain business at first but now I don't!"

Whirl-Fire was enraged. "VAIN? How dare you!" she cried. She stomped her hoof near Inferno. "You've probably wrecked my cave with your pathetic powers! Wait till my sister arrives and we'll show you what powers are!"

Inferno looked hurt and angry as he ran into the darkest corner of the rainforest.

Emily turned around to see Lily, Isla, Victoria, Jessica, and June running away, and that made Emily wonder what they were doing.

"Wild-Wind! For goodness' sake, come join me! Whatever you're doing, it can wait!" Whirl-Fire called to the air around her. Emily was confused. Who's she talking to? *There's no one here.*

As if answering her question, another Flash-Hoof Pony magically appeared beside Thunder. It was, Emily thought, perhaps Wild-Wind. As she started to run towards Whirl-Fire, she sent a quick smile to Thunder.

But Wild-Wind was so fast that Emily thought she must have imagined that smile.

"Wild-Wind, hurry!" Whirl-Fire snapped at her sister, glaring at everyone. "Let's get to the Crown Building so we can end this ridiculous obsession of pets," agreed Wild-Wind. She looked like she was forcing herself to act nasty. She reared up and sped towards the Crown building with her sister. Emily urged Thunder to run, but Whirl-Fire and Wild-Wind were faster than a flash of lightning. Still, Thunder didn't give up. He whinnied and soon, he galloped faster and faster.

He had almost caught up to the ponies when Emily grew a little anxious. Still, she encouraged him. "Keep on going, Thunder!"

Thunder started to pant but didn't give up. He increased his speed and quickly overtook the ponies, stopping near the Crown Building. Emily gasped in delight. She wasn't so overjoyed to see her horse overtake a record-breaking pony as much, but she was delighted to know that she could save the school now.

Suddenly, a yellow flash of sunlight appeared right in front of Thunder. The light dissolved after a few seconds, and there, standing beside Thunder, were Sparkle, Tisa, Rocket, Moon, and Saturn. "We are helping you fight the evil ponies," whispered Moon and Sparkle at the same time.

"Sure. Thanks," Emily said. Moon whinnied as she struck her hooves on the ground. She was about to fly when the Flash-Hoof Ponies charged at her and the others.

As quick as lightning, Moon spread her wings along with Rocket and they both flew high in the sky, slowing the Ponies down by their wingbeats. The unicorns, below the pegasi, cantered at the two Flash-Hooves. None of this was scaring Whirl-Fire, nor her sister.

"Come on, Emily," said Thunder. "They're really close to destroying the school—at least the Crown Building at the moment—but we can't let that happen! I know you're with me, and I bet you know that I've got your back, too. And since we're both together, nothing can stop us from saving our Academy!"

Thunder's words melted all of Emily's nervousness. Now, she felt excited and light. "I am ready! Let's go!"

At the speed of a rocket, Thunder started to gallop. He ran around Whirl-Fire, blocking her view so she won't be able to focus.

"Stop!" snarled Whirl-Fire. "Wild-Wind, do something!" But her sister didn't move.

"No, I'm not going to stop," said Thunder bluntly. He whispered to Emily, "Get off my back. Trust me."

Emily obediently got off her horse's back. Thunder reared and struck his hoof at Whirl-Fire's hind leg. She whined and her eyes glowed green, but she fell to her knees. Getting up quickly, Whirl-Fire tried to power-up her flame-made horn to blast fire on everyone, but Emily jumped in time and flung herself onto Whirl-Fire.

"What are you doing?" snarled Whirl-Fire.

"This," said Emily, putting her palms over Whirl-Fire's eyes. Whirl-Fire grew agitated. She moved here and there, trying to throw Emily off, but Emily wouldn't budge. Emily suddenly had a plan. "Shh, Whirl!" she whispered in the pony's ear. "I totally get why you hate pets, because I . . . er, do too. Humans . . . um, pamper them so much, don't they? I can't believe my parents got me a horse and sent me off to this school. And I'm honestly on your side."

Whirl-Fire stopped and listened, a wicked smile stretching across her face.

"I'll help you destroy the Crown Building," she continued in whispers. "You're not facing the building. Turn a little."

Whirl-Fire turned.

Emily slid off the pony in a hurry. "Now charge in and don't open your eyes, because such nasty things about the rainforest are written in the Academy that if you read them, you'd be terrified for life!"

Whirl-Fire had been in the direction of building earlier, but now had changed direction and was facing the rainforest. She sprinted closer to the rainforest and then stopped. The horses cornered her as she opened her eyes and neighed in rage.

"I'm right here, Emily," said Thunder. Emily

climbed on her horse and hugged him. Together, they ran away and stopped at a good distance from Whirl-Fire.

"Thunder," whispered Emily, "I know what to do!" She clapped her heels gently on Thunder's sides, so he ran over to the ponies. Whirl-Fire and Wild-Wind were at the Crown Building. All Emily had was a piece of a shattered rock. She studied it closely. Then, showing it to Thunder and getting his approval, she cried, "If you don't move . . ."

Whirl-Fire tensed. With an angry look in her eyes, she and Wild-Wind charged to the back door of the Crown Building. Emily expected Thunder to run after Whirl, but he began to pant. "I'm tired," he said.

Emily stroked his mane. "We can't give up. The school and everyone in it is in danger."

Thunder got up in an instant. "You are right," he said, determined. "I have a plan. Let's tell our friends to corner Whirl-Fire and Wild-Wind. You and I will lock the back door stealthily. Then, as our friends corner the two Flash-Hooves, let's drive them further into the rainforest with the help of the whole school and deal with them there."

Emily's eyes widened. "And if they try to threaten us with their flame horns, I know what to do!"

Emily and Thunder ran to tell their friends the plan. After a lot of yeses, Emily urged Thunder to run to the Crown Building. "Left!" she cried, as she saw Whirl-Fire and Wild-Wind cantering towards the Crown Building. Thunder and the rest of Rainbow Crown took the left side as others took different sides of the Crown Building. Fiercely, Whirl-Fire reared, but Thunder was a brave horse. He reared, too, his eyes flashing.

Emily leapt off Thunder, shaking with anger. Fiercely determined to protect the Academy and everyone in it, she and Thunder ran forward, charging after Whirl-Fire and Wild-Wind into the rainforest. Suddenly Wild-Wind stopped, her horn ablaze, pointing it towards Thunder. Emily dropped to her knees and picked up some dry sand. She threw it at Wild-Wind's horn, so the flames went out. Looking defeated, Wild-Wind fled away, trying to stop her horn's flames from sizzling away.

Whirl-Fire watched aghast as her sister was defeated. She dug a little hole in the sand with her hoof nervously, speechless, her mouth open like a goldfish. Whirl-Fire stared at Emily, unsure of what to do. She then slowly backed a few steps from the Crown Building and began to think of her next step.

Emily caught her breath as she watched the Ponies flee into the rainforest, the Terplantatious following close behind on a ramp of slippery ice. There was a moment's silence. Emily tensed for a second, wondering if the ponies would come back. But the silence continued. The Ponies had definitely left.

"They're gone!" she finally cried. "The school is safe! Everyone's safe!" She threw her arms in the air and whooped, and was quickly followed by the rest of the students.

"Woo-hoo!" exclaimed Rainbow Crown,

high-fiving. "You did it!"

"Go Emily! Go Thunder!" Ivy whooped.

"It wouldn't have been possible without you," Emily whispered to Thunder.

He nuzzled her. "Or you, Emily."

"Group hug!" Isla squealed. The girls and pets of Rainbow Crown embraced tightly.

As the girls pulled away, they all heaved a sigh of relief and high-fived once more. "Hey, where do think the princi—" Emily began but paused when she heard hoofbeats and footsteps. Who could it be? "Rainbow Crown!" cried Angel's familiar voice. Principal Pegasus cantered towards them. "What is going on?"

"Principals! I'm sorry, but, well, it's a long story," Ivy said.

"Then you need not recount it," Starlight whickered, trotting forward. "We saw what was going on. Part of it, anyway."

Emily beamed.

"But, as much as we were worried and were ready to jump in and save you all, we trusted you all deeply and decided you didn't need anybody to save you. We thought that we might as well leave saving the Academy to our students," finished Feather warmly.

"We also trusted the locks of the detention room deeply, which is where we hid," Starlight chipped in, cheerfully.

The teachers and principals looked around at Rainbow Crown and smiled. "You've been very smart and brave today. We're all so proud," said Angel.

"Indeed!" Silky agreed.

"And, Thunder and Emily, you seemed to have encouraged all your friends to stop the creatures," Starlight pointed out. "You both played a big role in saving the school. Thank you."

Emily's heart fluttered happily hearing all the praises that came her, Thunder's, and her friends' way.

"Well," said Angel at last, "it's getting late, isn't it?"

"I suppose it is," Starlight's eyes shone. "How does a special, all-Crown buffet dinner sound?"

Emily squealed with delight. "What? Really? Amazing! Wow! Awesome!"

"Oh, and of course," Angel smiled, "the horses may use the gazebo by the pool in my yard if they wish." She paused as Thunder reared up in joy.

"Can we?" he neighed. "Please?"
"How can we say no?" Feather beamed, wagging her tail.

Soon, Rainbow Crown was sitting merrily in the biggest lounge in the Crown Building, which was right on top. Everyone enjoyed the hot tomato soup, spaghetti Bolognese, tea cakes, and coconut marshmallow ice-cream for dinner, organized specially with the other Crowns.

Rainbow Crown was sitting at a table with Magic and Shimmer Crown, much to their delight.

"Mm, I love marshmallows," said a girl called Elizabeth, in between bites of her ice-cream. Her puppy hopped onto her lap. "And you were really the shining star today, Emily."

"Aw, thank you!"

"Hey, everyone?" said Lily. "You do know that we've solved this and all, but we still haven't . . . fixed it. I say we find a way to do so!"

Chapter 15

Mystery Solved!

"So that's why there was a tunnel!" Emily gasped. "Don't you see? The animals must have built it—"

"Because they needed to get into the Academy without anyone seeing," Abby finished. "They needed a secret way to get in!"

"Yep, makes sense," Isla high-fived her. "I also think they made holes in the race-course to purposely frighten the horses."

"Why?" asked Ivy.

"Because they hate pets!"

"Why?"

"Maybe they feel our pets are too pampered?"

"Why?"

"Because I sort of feel they are."

"Why?"

"Because the only thing I've been asked for one minute straight is 'why'."

"Okay."

"Hey, but one time I tried to get in, the tunnel was sealed! I think that's because a creature must have been in there!" Emily added.

"I'm just glad we're safe now," Ivy said, sipping her hot chocolate. "All's well that ends well, I guess."

Isla looked surprised hearing Ivy say that. "We are not safe," she said immediately. "The animals may come back. And we need to seal the rainforest," Isla said, looking like she would have sealed the rainforest right then. She sprang out of her seat, soup spilling on her culottes. "I'm on it!"

Emily facepalmed. "Isla really wants to seal that rainforest!"

After around ten minutes of waiting silently, the girls heard footsteps. "The building's locked," Isla panted. She told her friends that, knowing what had happened, the teachers had locked the

Crown Building and the stables for everyone's safety.

"But I'm not going to stop!" Isla said. "I'm telling the rainforest security to seal the rainforest. Now!" Ivy and Lily looked unhappy. "Really?" Ivy wondered aloud. "No, I think Honey was right. We should resolve this by making friends with the creatures in the rainforest."

"I agree," Emily said. "Because, no offense, Isla, but your plan won't work."

Isla's eyebrows rose.

"We don't have security in the rainforest."

"I also agree about the friendship bit," Ivy said.

Lily nodded in agreement. "Definitely!" she said happily. "Let's leave a note. We really owe a lot to Emily. In fact, why don't you drop the letter off, Emily? We'll write it, and if you like, you can add something."

Emily blushed. "I-I'm not that brave. I can be

brave at times though. I'll let Thunder do the drop-off."

"Yes, let Thunder do it," said Lily. "Now, I bet all the rainforest animals will be our friends. I noticed that some of them had smiled at us."
"Okay. But Emily, I—we—are eternally grateful," River said warmly.

Emily turned redder. "Oh thanks, River." She yawned. "What time is it? Oh my! It's late!"

Everyone nodded. "See you all tomorrow! Let's go to our Diamonds," Emily said.

Emily plopped on her bed and closed her eyes. After one hour, she heard an owl's hoot. It was so loud, like the owl was in her own room! She stirred a little, stretched, and sat upright. She slid off her bed and, just for fun, pranced around her Diamond. Her green-brown eyes caught sight of the picture of her and Thunder. Thunder would love a gallop under the stars, wouldn't he? thought Emily with a wide grin. He doesn't like sleeping, as—whenever he is in his stall—he's always thinking about races and being outdoors. Thunds would simply adore running in the dark, taking in all the fresh scents of flowers and galloping through open fields. Her grin grew bigger. *I'll go ask him! What a fabulous treat!*

Getting her hopes higher, Emily put the photo down. She rushed to her door, but then remembered the building was locked. She slumped on her bed and then scrambled to the window, gazing at the stars she wanted to ride under. Suddenly, as she took one final round about her room, she caught sight of a yellow-and-pink stick-like thing, folded up in a corner of her room. Emily ran to it. There was something written on it: "Fold-Up Ladder". She gasped in excitement and took it to her window, where—after she opened it—she let the ladder unravel, rung by rung, step by step. Soon she heard a thud and knew she could now climb down.

Reaching the bottom, Emily jumped off the ladder and zipped off to the stables. As she reached there, and her eyes adjusted to the dark, she saw a rather interesting sight.

Her horse was half out of the window, half in, snoring loudly.

"Hey! Thunder," Emily hissed, chuckling. "Wake up!"

Thunder cocked his head in his sleep. "Hmm," he mumbled sleepily. "Hmm! Oh, hello!"

"Hey!" Emily grinned.

"Oh, the eggs are alive? The milkshake is asleep, you say?" Thunder babbled.

"Um, not really. But dinner was great!"

"Wrap it in the cake . . ."

"Are you talking in your sleep?"

"I'm not walking to weep," Thunder murmured, still fast asleep.

"Thunder!" Emily exclaimed, opening his eyes with her fingers.

"Oh! Emily! You want something? I have plenty of alive eggs and sleeping milkshakes. Or . . . now that I think of it, I think that might have been a dream . . ."

"I've heard enough of the eggs and milk now, Thunds," said Emily with a chuckle, "and I didn't want anything, let alone your famous 'alive eggs'. But I was just wondering what this . . . posture is about." Her eyes glimmered with excitement. "What have you been up to, to achieve this pose?"

"Trying to get out," Thunder explained. "The stables are locked."

"O . . . kay," Emily said, stifling a giggle. "Dinner was really good."

Thunder nickered. "Mine too! Saturn, Victoria's unicorn, is really nice. I never knew how cool music spells were until he played my favourite song." "I'm asking him to enchant my radio!" Emily said with a grin. "Well, as tomorrow is Sunday, I was thinking, how about we sleep under the stars tonight?"

Thunder whinnied. "Yes! I'd love to! But first, please let me go for a canter. Please?"

Emily nodded, "Okay, sure. I'll ride with you, too!"

Thunder looked puzzled. "But aren't you afraid of riding?"

Emily looked thoughtful, "No, I think I'll get over that soon."

Thunder smiled. "Then let's go!" He squeezed out of the window and began trotting with Emily. Then Emily climbed onto him, and they took a nice, long ride around the stables. After half an hour or so, Thunder lay down on some fresh, soft grass alongside Emily.

After hearing many parrot calls, Emily slowly opened her eyes and saw the sun rising. She shielded her eyes from its beautiful and bright rays. "Thunder!" she whispered. Her horse stood up and stretched.

"Emily!" Thunder smiled. "Good morning!" He tossed his tangled mane and his eyes twinkled merrily. Emily hugged Thunder and stroked his mane. She suddenly heard a buzz and some pop music. A scroll was flying straight towards her! It landed with a plop and Emily hurriedly picked it up, saying, "What is this?"

The note read,

Dear Emily,
You are going to receive the letter to give to the rainforest animals in a minute. Saturn, in the stables, heard you talking to Thunder, so I set this whole thing up to make it easy.

Love,
Victoria and Saturn
PS. I'm sorry that you can hear heavy pop music. Saturn is doing Music Magic so we can't do anything (so far) without some music.

Emily giggled, showed the scroll to Thunder,

and then put it in her pocket. She stroked Thunder and said, "Let's go for a canter, now that the sun is out."

Thunder started to trot with Emily on his back. Soon, they passed several patches of flowers and even spotted some cute rabbits. Emily carried one in her hands. "Hi," she cooed. "I'll call you Chloe. I'll come to feed you every day with Thunder!"

The bunny looked happy and nuzzled against Emily. Emily looked puzzled. "Thunder, what is the bunny trying to say?" she whispered.

Thunder smiled and replied, "She's saying that she would love to stay with you because she usually feels lonely out here."

Emily cuddled Chloe, then put her gently down.

Suddenly, Thunder reared and caught a scroll that played rock music. Emily smiled and told Thunder about the plan to drop off the note. "You can," she said generously.

"We can," Thunder declared with a smile.

"You're so sweet. Only if you're there, I will." Emily kissed his rose-scented mane and opened the scroll.

To the Rainforest Creatures,

We know we tried to defeat you, but we just have a heart for domestic pets, too. We believe we can all be one. One glowing circle of friends. If you accept this letter, we will not seal the rainforest. We really hope you accept this and come to the Academy one day soon. Think: wouldn't it be lovely for us to like each other?

Emily saw Thunder's face soften as he read. Pulling a pencil out of her pocket, Emily added something.

Hopefully friends,
Emily, Victoria, Ivy, Lily, Abby, Isla
Students of the Animal Academy

Thunder added his and the rest of the pets' names.

Taking a deep, slightly trembly breath, Emily got onto Thunder with the note. They hastily walked to the rainforest.

"Stop!" cried Emily all of a sudden. "I'm not brave enough." She leant forward to feel Thunder's mane on her face.

"Yes, you are," Thunder said firmly.

Emily sighed. "Thank you, thank you. Now let's drop that note off!" They cantered the rest of the way. When they reached, the rainforest was eerily quiet. The only noise was Thunder's cautious hoofbeats. Emily's heart clenched, frightened, as a ghostly mist swept over them. "We have to turn back . . ." Emily's voice quivered as Thunder trotted further into the rainforest. She got off Thunder and timidly walked to a cave. She sat on a rock next to it. "Where do we put the note?" she asked, shivering. It was getting colder by the second.

"Here," Thunder nudged on a tree's root that was covered in moss. "They'll see it here." Emily glanced around before tiptoeing to it and dropping the note on it.

Please. Please work, she willed anxiously. The mist was getting thicker, and Emily's vision was narrowing. Now, she could only see the things five steps away from her. She glanced at the cave near the tree. It didn't look like it was inhabited. She darted in there with Thunder walking warily behind. But as soon as they set foot in there . . . the ground gave way!

Emily and Thunder both tumbled into a tiny pit. "Where are we?" breathed Emily, feeling around. She looked up and at the walls. The pit wasn't all that tall, so she could easily climb out.

The tree's root, the one on which the letter had been kept, throbbed, and moved with great force. Emily and Thunder began to yell frantically. The tree shook violently as its main root almost cracked. The ground quaked as enormous branches hurtled down, almost like a trap. "Help!" Emily shouted, scrambling out of the pit. She ran with Thunder following her.

They were all alone! A vine caught on Thunder's hoof, making him tumble to the ground.

As Thunder fell to his knees, the vine snapped, awakening four families of white bellbirds who screeched deafeningly as they fled. Emily covered her ears as the birds shrieked, but their cacophonous noise wasn't anything compared to the sound of her heart beating.

Thunder scrambled back up and glanced around. The mist was disappearing. Just as he and Emily

decided to gallop back, footsteps rang behind them. Turning sharply around, Emily saw dark figures approaching them.

"Leave," a deep, familiar voice growled. "NOW." Emily yelped and clutched Thunder's tail.

But before they could flee, Emily saw a figure stomp its foot. There was a crack, and everything turned white!

Emily stood absolutely still. Taking a deep breath, she looked left to see Thunder but all was white. She could see nothing.

Run, Emily's instincts screamed. Just as she was about to sprint, mist and fog fell on her like a thick duvet. Emily tried to break free, but it just circled around her, hissing and bubbling. Suddenly, she saw a pair of hooves burst through. Something was punching at the cloud cover. The air was still white, but Emily knew in her heart that it was Thunder. For him, anything was possible.

The mist gradually died down, fluttering away slowly like a blanket of white feathers. Thunder and Emily bolted towards a dense, dark grove of trees. The fog disappeared as soon as the two were hidden safely to reveal evil Whirl-Fire, the Terplantatious, and other scowling, wicked Flash-Hoof ponies. They sniffed the ground as Whirl-Fire exited her cave. It looked like the other animals were her helpers.

Emily and Thunder listened carefully, hiding behind the grove shelter.

"If that small cub Inferno was here," Wild-Wind grumbled, "we could have made him sniff this out." The Terplantatious, in spite, sent a freezing light and froze a gecko who was hunting a fly. It froze, tongue poked out. "I knew we should have put a harder spell on him; Inferno got away too easily," he fussed.

Emily peeked out from a creeper, seeing several rainforest animals near where the note was.

Whirl-Fire stomped on the ground, exasperated. "Well? I knew that those Animal Academy humans would come to seal the rainforest. But we are too smart for their tricks. We—"

Wild-Wind, her sister, interrupted. "A scroll!" she exclaimed.

All the animals crowded around Wild-Wind. Their faces began to crack like a boiled egg into a smile. Even Whirl-Fire's! Taking a deep breath, Thunder stepped boldly out.

He neighed shyly, and everyone's head whipped around. Whirl-Fire reared violently. Then she paused, seeing the trust and compassion in Thunder's eyes. She stopped in her tracks, and her wicked neigh turned into a happy one.

"Whirl?" said Thunder timidly. "I hope you accept the letter."

The pony smiled a little and then turned to her cave and strutted away. Emily stroked Thunder's mane. "We've done all we could. Let's give them time to think," she whispered. Her eyes shimmered and Thunder whinnied delightedly. Their ride back from the rainforest was peaceful. Butterflies flew by, the ponds rippled, fish leapt in and out, and Emily beamed at the thought of all the animals uniting.

"You did it!" a squeal rang out. It was Isla, and the rest of Rainbow Crown and their pets! "We did it," Thunder beamed, holding a proud

look. "Never imagined that I'd ever see the Flash-Hoof Pony smile."

Everyone heaved a sigh of relief. "Yay!" said Ivy, smiling. She hugged Emily. "I knew you could do it!"
"Let's wait. They might come," decided Abby.

"Hang on!" Emily said suddenly, remembering something important.

Everyone stopped chattering and listened. "What?" asked Isla and Lily at the same time.

"The Terplantatious said something about spells. He said that Inferno should have had a harder spell on him. Does that mean we might need a spell to break the evilness of the creatures?" Emily said.

"Hmm . . ." Abby murmured. "Good point."

Emily nodded. "Okay." And before anyone could say anything else, she ran to Starlight Silverwave's stable.

"Hello, Starlight," said Emily. "I have a request. You are the best at magic. Will you please use it on the rainforest creatures?"

Starlight looked firm. "Rainforest creatures? We shall seal the rainforest and that's all."

Emily's eyes widened. "Please, don't . . ." she said. Quickly she explained what she and her friends had done. Starlight gasped. "Wow, Emily! That was tremendously brave of you, of all of you," she said.

"What shall I do?"

Emily told Starlight about the Terplantatious talking about a spell. "I feel if you cast a spell of goodness on them," Emily said, "they'll be forced to be happy. So maybe you could just break the evil spell?"

"Oh, Emily," Starlight said, looking at her student. "Your efforts will not be in vain, promise. But do you think we should force the animals to be happy and to smile their whole entire life? They too are animals—living beings—and they should be able to choose how they feel and how to express it. Yet, I believe you when you say the animals are cursed with a spell and it should be broken. But let's not break it with a spell, shall we, and instead use the magic of companionship?"

Starlight's words got Emily thinking. She believed Starlight's every word and agreed with it.

The unicorn continued, "All the animals at the school have such close bonds with their human friends, and they're not like that due to a magic spell. The same could be with the creatures of the rainforest."

Emily bit her lip. "That's true. I'll go to the rainforest with Thunder. Tisa is right! The friendship between animals and their owners is stronger than an evil spell! Oh, thank you, thank you!"

Starlight beamed.

Soon, Thunder and Emily were in the rainforest. "Whirl-Fire?" Thunder called from the threshold of the rainforest. "We—"

"Flash-Hoof ponies! Terplantatious! Hi!" Emily interrupted, looking further in. What was that? All the animals raced to them, grinning from ear to ear.

"We read your letter," Wild-Wind said merrily. "It taught us a better way of... being with people. No one has ever asked us to be friends with them before. Thank you for writing the scroll. And by the way, my name is Sunrise." Her eyes looked sad.

"We were named evil names too, by Ra . . . um
. . . somebody," she said, hesitating. "Inferno's
name is Periwinkle and the Terplantatious'
name is Opal."

Whirl-Fire grinned, nuzzling her sister affectionately.
"My name is Candlelight. Candlelight Glow
Flash." She put a hoof on Emily and drew her
in for a hug.Emily beamed wider than ever
possible. She flung her arms around Candlelight
and hugged back. "I'm so glad you're good," she
exclaimed.

"I'm so glad you don't hate me," said Candlelight.
"I'd never hate you now," Emily said.

Emily walked back to the school grounds with
Thunder and the rainforest animals, where all
the Crowns were standing and playing. The
students of the Academy, their pets, and the
rainforest animals mingled with one another.
After a while, Thunder cantered over to Emily
with Candlelight. "I'm playing this awesome
game with the Flash-Hoof Ponies. We race five
times and whoever wins the most can ask the
others for a wish!"

"The only things we asked for were apples and water because we were so hungry!" Thunder said and then galloped away.

Emily now looked at Candlelight shyly. "Ah!" said Candlelight, as if remembering something. She took out a heart-shaped ruby from a magical floating shield. "Here," she said, eyes glimmering softly. "This is my lucky ruby. I want you to have it because I'm good again, and it's all because of you. Thank you!"

"No, thank you, Candlelight!" cried Emily happily, feeling the gem in her hands. "It's so pretty."

"Thanks! I know what you're thinking, and no. It has no powers. I mean, it's the Ruby of Love, so maybe it gives out love," Candlelight giggled.

Thunder came cantering back and smiled energetically at Candlelight. He said, "All the rainforest animals promised that they would help the school from now on! Amazing, isn't it!" Emily's heart glowed with happiness. They seemed much safer with the rainforest creatures protecting them!

Emily vaulted onto Thunder as they galloped across the grass, past the rainforest, and into the beautiful meadow to the north of the Academy. Emily's face lit up as she rode, laughing happily as she felt the cool breeze whooshing past her. She hugged Thunder, feeling like she was on cloud nine.

She looked up at the sky, which glistened with pink, gold, and orange.

Thunder slowed to a trot as they reached the top of a hill. "Best friends!" they chorused happily, galloping up a hill and stopping at it. As they smiled, a shooting star glided across the sky, leaving gold shimmers twinkling magically. "With you, there's always magic," said Emily, smiling lovingly.

"And with you, too," Thunder said nuzzling Emily's hair and grinning affectionately.

"You're the best friend I could ever ask for."

"Partners always and forever!" Emily exclaimed. "Always and forever!" Thunder whinnied, his eyes shining brightly.

They hugged each other in adoration.

Emily's eyes met Thunder's and both of them smiled, the setting sun sparkling. The sun's dazzling beams illuminated the sky as Emily bounced off Thunder's back, giving him another tight hug. The two beamed at each other adoringly. Emily's heart glowed as she and Thunder gazed at the sun, it's light shimmering magically as it set in the horizon.

Acknowledgements

Hey there – it's me, Riah!

I'm delighted you took time out to read this page, because that means I get to tell you about all the people who helped make this book come to life.

First, though – I really hope that you enjoyed reading this book as much as I enjoyed writing it! (And trust me, I had the best time ever writing and editing Rainforest Rescue.) But I couldn't have published it without the support of many people.

I could not have undertaken this excellent journey without my Mum and Dad, who believed in me no matter what. Mum, Dad, you both really deserve to be crowned "Most Encouraging Parents"! And words cannot express how grateful I am to have my four grandparents as my biggest cheerleaders ever. I'm extremely grateful to Shikha Masi and Gaurav Mama who encouraged me to publish this book and helped me in the process of doing so.

I would like to express my deepest gratitude to Garima Shukla, my editor with whom I enjoyed many lighthearted moments over hours of phone calls. I had immense pleasure collaborating with Shalini Soni, my illustrator, who turned my words into stunning drawings. A big thank you to Payal Jaipuria for her hard work and coordination, and to Prashant Pathak for his support and encouragement.

A big shout out to my awesome best friends – Samara, Sophie, Ishanvi, Aanika, Aarna, Aditi, Leah, Aanvi, Ahana, Divyana, and Ryka. All of you went out of your way to ask how my book-writing process was going. You inspired the girls in Animal Academy too – your humor and tall tales (thanks, Sophie!) inspired Isla, and all of your supportiveness and kindness inspired Emily's best friends. Samara and Aanika, thank you so much for your daily dose of encouragement!

My dearest teachers – Ms. Beveridge, Ms. Shukla, Ms. Mehta, Ms. Prasad, Ms. Velati, Ms. Chawla, Ms. Irani, and Ms. Bhatia – thank you for teaching me everything I needed to write this book, from how to recite the alphabet to how to use figurative language. Mrs. Talpade, Mrs. Lele, and Mrs. Ganguly, thank you for initiating my adoration for books – from book fairs at school, to our annual novel study, and from author talks to well-stocked libraries.

I'd like to thank the three who inspired this series – my amazing Shih Tzu, Tisa, for being a cute (but a little grumpy) cuddle toy and a best friend who barks really loudly. Not to forget, the two cats who inspired the series – Leo and Xena. From the day I found them in a garden near my house during lockdown in 2021, till now!

And finally, to whoever is reading this – thank you for picking this book up and reading it. With your support and encouragement, the series Animal Academy can grow faster, and you'll have more books to read really soon!

Riah

About The Author

Riah Rajani is a ten-year-old story writer, the author of the whimsical book Animal Academy. She lives in the vibrant, bustling city of Mumbai, with her family, her Shih Tzu puppy Tisa, and her cats Xena and Leo.

Her love for these three spirited animals and the time she spends with them in the gardens and promenades next to her home led to the concept of Animal Academy.

If Riah is not happily reading books, she is almost always walking her pup, travelling, sketching imaginative drawings, listening to music, playing around with quirky photo filters, or hanging out with her friends and family.